SALVATION ARMY

SEMIOTEXT(E) NATIVE AGENTS SERIES

Cet ouvrage, publié dans le cadre d'un programme d'aide à la publication, bénéficie du soutien financier du ministère des Affaires étrangères, du Service culturel de l'ambassade de France aux Etats-Unis, ainsi que de l'appui de FACE (French American Cultural Exchange).

This work, published as part of a program providing publication assistance, received financial support from the French Ministry of Foreign Affairs, the Cultural Services of the French Embassy in the United States and FACE (French American Cultural Exchange).

Published by Semiotext(e)
2007 Wilshire Blvd., Suite 427, Los Angeles, CA 90057
www.semiotexte.com

"Cette traduction est dediée à toi, Bob Whiteman: Tu m'aimes, donc, je suis."
—Frank Stock

Special thanks to Clélia Casagrande, Robert Dewhurst, Ariana Reines, Michael Silverblatt, and Noura Wedell.

Cover Photography: Ulf Andersen/Gamma
Back Cover Photography: Abdellah Taïa by Ulf Andersen
Design: Hedi El Kholti
French Voices Logo designed by Serge Bloch

ISBN: 978-1-58435-070-5
Distributed by The MIT Press, Cambridge, Mass. and London, England
Printed in the United States of America

10 9 8 7 6 5 4 3 2

SALVATION ARMY

a novel

Abdellah Taïa

Introduction by Edmund White

Translated from the French by Frank Stock

\<e\>

For Mohamed, my father

Introduction by Edmund White

Love and Loneliness—

Abdellah Taïa's *Salvation Army*

This is a novel about love in all its forms. A Moroccan boy's love for his mother. That woman's love for her husband, despite the violence of his passion, the stinging ardor of his jealousy. The boy's love for his older brother, for the traces of sperm on his underpants, for his kindness and remoteness, for his bookishness, for his womanizing, for his gentle help.

This is a book about love, about a boy's love of his family, as intertwined as a pack of dogs, as intimate and snarling and cozy, all imbued with the same enticing smell. About the boy's love of the French language and literature, which he is determined to master though he can't really afford to buy books, though his native language is Arabic. This is, almost parenthetically, a book about the love of men for men, about anonymous sex in the Geneva public toilets or the sudden, quick threesome shared with a young Pole and a young German on a train bound for Madrid.

This is a novel about a boy's love for his past, for his great tribe of an extended family, for the look and variety and tastes and bedeviling charms of Morocco, this country so vast and incomprehensible that he puts its name in quotation marks ("Morocco") as if it truly exists only on posters aimed at tourists, as an abstraction despite its very real and disparate pleasures.

This is also a novel about fear. A young Moroccan arrives in Geneva to finish his studies at the university and the middle-aged Swiss academic who has invited him to live with him isn't there. The Moroccan (the narrator of the book) has no money and no place to go. Fortunately he is told by a kindly stranger to go to the Salvation Army, where he's given a bed by a man who resembles Michel Foucault and who is absorbed by his reading of Benjamin Constant's great novel of passion, *Adolphe*.

Everything in this book is odd, even the administrator at the university in charge of his dossier, an alcoholic woman who is by turns giddy with merriment and erupting into fierce rages. The Moroccan sits on a park bench, a quickie sex partner gives him an orange to eat, he takes a sip from a fountain—and recognizes it as a Wallace fountain from his French textbooks about Paris. If the secret to great fiction, as the Russian Formalists argued, is *defamiliarization*, making everything known seem strange, then nothing could be more accomplished and persuasive than this mysterious novel. The boy himself is foreign to us, our world is foreign to him, everyone is a foreigner in love with the "other" (whether that be a Swiss man or an older brother).

This is a book about someone at a moment of transition between being a nice Moroccan boy, one of nine children, someone enamored of his own parents and big brother, a good kid—and becoming a French intellectual, a Parisian and a published novelist. Despite the extreme simplicity and clarity of Taïa's style, we sense how sophisticated he is—that this is a simplicity that only intelligence and experience and wide reading in several languages can buy. Not only has the language been chastened, but the selection of scenes to show and to exclude has also been subjected to a draconian editing process.

Finally, this is a book about poverty. About sexual tourism, its benign side (an older Swiss man offers a Moroccan boy the chance to escape his milieu and to realize his fantasies) and its cruel side (the same Swiss man casually, greedily, buys the favors of another Moroccan while on holiday). The boy is proud, quick, adaptable, almost feminine in his desire to please, boyish in his enthusiasm and trusting nature—but he is also without resources, easy to manipulate, terribly easy to exploit. I'm convinced that there is an up side to every human relationship, even pedophilia and sexual tourism, but only in one case out of a hundred. In all the other ninety-nine cases there is finally nothing but an abuse of power, a deforming imbalance of wealth, a facility on the part of the First World tourist for forgetting that the young person from the Third World is also a human being, not just a "cheap whore" (to use the language repeatedly on the lips of the Swiss man, Jean). Money is an obsession in a third world country such as Morocco where the average wage is miniscule and a man feels like a man only when he can bring home a basket full of vegetables and meat.

But the people in the First World also know perfectly well the impact of their purchasing power. They know how to buy another human being, or how to "rent" him, even though these crude transactions are disguised as acts of friendship. The Swiss don't go to Germany as sexual tourists, after all; no, they go to North Africa or Southeast Asia. Sex in these cases is all about money, about the exchange rate, about trading certain numbers (age, waist size, penis size, income size) for other numbers.

But Abdellah Taïa doesn't spell all this out. His is an ecstatic and generous nature who lives in the particular, who shies away from generalizations. He accepts each person into his life not as a representative but as a unique individual. No matter how often he might be disappointed or wounded, he is ever an optimist and prepared to receive that wonderful, transforming thing: reciprocal affection. This book is a clear stream; drink from it deeply.

I

She always slept with us, in the middle, between my little brother Mustapha and my sister Rabiaa.

She would fall asleep very quickly, and night after night, her snoring would punctuate her sleep in a natural, almost harmonious manner. It used to bother us in the beginning, keep us from a peaceful entry into dreams. Over time, her nocturnal music, her noises, became a benevolent breathing that accompanied our nights and even reassured us when we were racked by nightmares that wouldn't let go until we were exhausted, wiped out.

For a long time, Hay Salam our house in Salé, was nothing more than a ground floor dwelling with three rooms, one for my father, one for my older brother Abdelkébir, and the last one for us, the rest of the family: my six sisters, Mustapha, my mother and I. In that room, there were no beds, just three benches that served as our living room couch during the day.

We spent all of our time in that room, where there was also this monstrous, gigantic old cupboard, all packed in together: we ate there, sometimes made mint tea, went over our lessons, entertained guests, told stories that never ended. And, yes, that's where we'd argue, politely or violently depending on the day, our mental state and, most importantly, our mother's reaction.

For several years, my childhood, my adolescence, the essential part of my life occurred in that room facing the street. Four walls that didn't really protect us from outside noises. A small roof to live under, storing in our memory, beneath our skin, what made up our life, experimenting everything, feeling everything and later, remembering it all.

The other two rooms were almost beyond limits, especially Abdelkébir's. He was the oldest, almost the king of the family. My father's room was at once the reception room, the library where he stored his magnificently-bound Arabic books, and his love nest. That's where my parents made love. And they did it at least once a week. We knew. We knew everything that happened at home.

To communicate his sexual desire to my mother, my father had perfected his own techniques, his own strategies. One of them consisted simply in spending the evening with us, in our room. My father, who was a great talker, who commented on everything, would suddenly fall silent. He would not say anything, no word or sound would cross his lips. He wouldn't even smoke. He'd huddle in a corner of the room, alone with the torments of his desire, in the first stages of the sex act, already in a state of pleasure, his arms around his body. His silence was eloquent, heavy, and nothing could break it.

My mother would get it pretty quickly, and so would we.

When she accepted his silent proposition, she'd enliven the evening with her village tales and outbursts of laughter. Tired, or angry, she would be silent as well. Her refusals were obvious, and my father would not insist. Once, upset, he took his revenge on her, and on us by the same token (although we maintained complete neutrality in terms of their sexual relations, or at least tried to) by cutting off the electricity to the entire house. He thus cruelly kept us from the international variety shows that we followed with great interest every week on television. He made us as frustrated as he was. Nobody complained. We understood perfectly: no pleasure for him, no pleasure for us.

M'Barka would wait until we were asleep before going to his reception room. She'd leave us then, her mind at ease, to carry out her conjugal duties and make her man happy. Several times I tried to stay awake to witness this magic moment: her heading out into the darkness towards love. In vain. Back then I had no trouble sleeping. I'd climb into bed and the darkness inside me would almost immediately become a movie screen. It was a talent I inherited from my mother.

On love-making nights, my mother's snoring was no longer there to accompany us, cradle us. To love us. Getting up the next day was hard, something was missing, but M'Barka would have already returned, in her spot, between Rabiaa and Mustapha.

My dreams at night weren't sexual. On the other hand, on certain days my imagination would easily, and with a certain level of arousal, tread on torrid and slightly incestuous ground. I would be in bed with my parents. My father inside my mother. My father's big, hard dick (it couldn't have been anything else but big!) penetrating my mother's enormous vagina. I'd hear their noise, their breath. At first, I wouldn't see anything, everything would be black, but eventually I'd be there beside them, closely watching these two bodies that I knew so well and at the same time didn't know. I'd be ready to lend a helping hand, aroused, happy and panting along with them. Mohamed would take M'Barka right away, sometimes without even undressing her. Their sexual coupling would last a long time, a very long time. They never spoke, and they always presented themselves to one another with their eyes closed. A perfect sexual harmony naturally achieved. They were made for one another, sex was clearly the preferred language through which the image of the couple they formed could be expressed. Even after bringing nine children into the world, their desire for one another remained intact, mysteriously and joyously intact.

In my mind, my family's reality has a strong sexual quality, it is as if we have all been one another's partners, we blended together ceaselessly, without guilt. Sex, regardless of who we have it with, should never scare us. My mother, her life, her pleasure and her tastes, has taught me this lesson I shall never forget and that I sometimes, naively, try to put into practice.

My parent's lovemaking nights often ended in a noisy uproar. My parents fought after sex. Noisily. Violently. It was always the same story, a story that never died.

My mother's screams, hysterical, possessed, beyond herself, would wake us up in the middle of the night.

"You're going to drive me crazy! I've sworn to this a hundred, a thousand times. He was here because of you, not because of me. He came to see you, not me. Don't you remember? Really? He wanted to ask you to help him cultivate his land. God! My God! How long do I have to put up with this, the pain, these accusations, always these same accusations? All my life? No, no, no … I've had enough, enough, enough … There are limits to what you can take. I can't put up with everything, take everything in. I'm not as strong as you think. How many more years is it going to take before you believe me? Why do I always have to justify myself? Why must I always go over the same things, the same story? You know that I've never been unfaithful to you, not with him, not with anybody. Do you want me to swear to that? Is that it? Anyway, I've already done that. It wouldn't phase me to do it again … Is that what you want? Don't come near me … No … Leave me alone. I've already given you what you wanted. My body belongs to you but that's no reason to mistreat it so. Why are you so hard on me all the time, what have I ever done to you? After all, I am the mother of your children, or have you forgotten that? … Be sensible! Think about God, think about the Prophet! All of that happened a long time ago, a very long time ago, almost in another lifetime … I don't even remember when, exactly, and what does it matter anyway … Don't come near me … Leave me alone … No, not the belt, you know you can't beat me, you're not that kind of man. Let me out of here … Let me leave … Help, help me!"

They had just gotten married. My father wasn't always home. He would look for work in the other villages. M'Barka would be alone for days at a time in the house at the Oulad Brahim settlement, not far from her brother-in-law's "farm." It wasn't a first marriage for either of them. Mohamed had been married to three other women before he met my mother. None of them seemed suitable to his sister Massouda, who made all his decisions for him. M'Barka was already a widow and the mother of a year old daughter when Mohamed showed up at her father's house to ask for her hand. Both of them had a good understanding of life and its pitfalls. They had already experienced love and its problems. Apparently, they couldn't be fooled by anything. Now they wanted a family, for real and for ever.

One day, Mohamed came home earlier than expected. It was market day, a Wednesday. He carried with him a basket full of vegetables and fresh fruit, red meat and mint. He was happy and proud. He would be with his wife again. He had earned some money. He felt like a man, M'Barka's man. Unfortunately for him, Saleh, my mother's cousin, was there, right in his own home. Even worse: He had also brought a basket crammed full of provisions. Mohamed had never been able to stand Saleh, that he found vulgar and spiteful. M'Barka and Saleh were sitting next to one another. Their knees were touching. They were drinking mint tea. They were laughing. They were almost playing make-believe, the way little kids play house. M'Barka slightly inched away from her cousin when Mohamed made his entrance. He noticed. He immediately concluded that something had gone on between them while he was gone. Their intimacy bothered him intensely, it immediately disgusted and sickened him. But he had to face this unpleasant surprise, this terrible situation, this doubt, the jealousy that sprang up when he surprised them sitting so close. And yet, he had to welcome Saleh, he was a relative. A member of the family that Mohamed not only didn't like but never invited over. Saleh took the liberty of making himself at home and that drove Mohamed crazy.

"*Salam alikoum*, cousin of my wife!"

"*Wa alikoum salam*, husband of my cousin!"

"You both seem happy … The neighbors could probably even hear you laughing … and suspect something fishÿ … especially since I am not supposed to be home."

"We've always been very close, M'Barka and I. We grew up together, played together, got into trouble together."

"And what made you laugh so loud? Tell me so I can laugh along with you!"

"Oh, this and that, anecdotes from the village … our childhood games, memories … Well, you know, the *douar* stories are so funny. M'Barka and I, we've gone through so much together, we could spend days on end going through our shared memories."

"Well, I see you don't need me, I'll leave you to your funny stories, leave your collusion intact … My head hurts, I'm going to bed. Goodbye."

Mohamed went into the bedroom, closed the windows violently and slammed the door. The message was clear. M'Barka took refuge in silence. Saleh left at once for his douar. He would never again come to visit his cousin in my father's house.

I never knew Saleh. Nevertheless, he was very much present in our lives. His name, very beautiful and sweet, still resonates in the Hay Salam house, because it was so often brought up, shouted, insulted, cursed. Saleh was the source of an absolute misunderstanding, a wound left open forever, a definitive sorrow. In my father's mind, it was a betrayal. The end of a certain idea of love and the start of an unbridled, violent sexuality without decency.

Since that cursed day, M'Barka never stopped justifying herself, never stopped telling her version of the story, explaining it, analyzing the smallest details, and, faced with my father's accusations, insisting on her "innocence" again and again. Mohamed discovered the world of jealousy which he would inhabit his whole life.

"No, no, and no ... I didn't sleep with Saleh. Never. Stop torturing me, smearing me like this in front of the children. What will the neighbors, good and bad, think of me now? They're going to tell themselves: Who would have believed that about her? Well, you know what they say: still water runs deep and dirty ... Me, a disgraced woman? A woman who deceives, a whore? Not on your life, do you hear me, do all of you hear me, no, not on your life! You don't believe me? Do you want me to swear on my father's soul? Is that what you want? What good will that do? I've already done that and it hasn't stopped you from bringing up your old accusation, from unsheathing your assassin's tongue, killing me slowly but surely … Well, maybe he wanted to fuck … but I didn't, not me, do you understand … Do you want me to say it again … NOT ME … I never gave him a chance to make advances, not him and not anybody else either … You are going to make me crazy … and you're crazy, crazy, crazy … Calm down … let your temper cool. Please, don't let the devil come between us, split us up. Think of our saint Sidi Moulay Brahim … Come here … Nothing ever happened … I swear on my father's soul. I would swear to it on Sidi Moulay Brahim's grave if that's what you wanted."

We would hear everything. M'Barka's loud voice filled every void and carried far, the smallest details of her story were revealed to all, to those nearby and to those far away, to friends as well as enemies. In the beginning, we didn't dare intervene, get involved in this story, so ancient, so intimate, so complicated. But when Mohamed took off his belt to beat M'Barka, at that very moment, alerted by my mother's terror-stricken cries, we'd all come running to her rescue. We would gather on the patio, red eyed, ashamed, frightened, on the verge of tears, trying to decide what to do. We were all afraid of the same thing, that he'd kill her in a fit of madness. Abdelkébir would try to force the door open. It was locked every time.

My mother would scream as if she were about to surrender her soul, as if my father were going to plunge that big knife used to sacrifice the sheep for Aïd el-Kébir into her heart, making our worst fears come true. We were always on the brink of tragedy. From drama to tragedy is a short step. Fortunately, the saints that M'Barka always invoked would finally intervene in our favor and grant us a portion of their peace.

M'Barka really knew how to wail and that was the right thing to do. That's what saved her every time.

Hysteria is an illness I know quite well.

Sometimes our nearest neighbors intervened as well. They would knock on the door and ask whoever answered: "What's going on with your mother? Is your father abusing her again?"

How could I respond to such hypocrisy? How could I defend my mother's honor? What could I say to these people who acted like our saviors and then, peddlers that they were, hastened to hawk the most ruinous gossip about our family?

No, my mother wasn't being abused by my father. Their love life was like that, complex, violent, tortured. True love, the kind that lasts and survives for years, is always full of passion and craziness. Mohamed never beat M'Barka. He just pretended, he knew he couldn't do it. He would raise his first, but he never brought it down. My mother, of course, exaggerated her screams to the utmost. A good comedienne, she knew everything about play-acting.

How could I get her out of there? How could I spring her from that prison and that paradise, yank her away from my father's furious jealousy, from that angel turned demon? How could I recover her safe and sound, and bring her back to our room, to us, to her place among us?

Without even thinking about it, we would all start banging on the door, crying, begging Mohamed to spare her this time, just this once. We pounded. We yelled too. And we always ended up breaking down the door, the door that had weakened over time, that had lost its center. A door with no guts, an empty frame. Then we'd find both of them, like two shameful kids caught playing some off-limits game, my father in his long johns, my mother almost naked beneath her transparent night-gown. Then Abdelkébir would save her. Mohamed would stay silent, letting his oldest son do what he had to do. Abdelkébir would fold M'Barka in his arms as if to cover her and would bring her back to our room. We'd form a procession behind them, and follow them into our room. A little while later, without a word, we would turn off the lights and pretend to sleep.

Silence again. A total silence, heavy, restless. Short lived.

In the dark, a few minutes after this temporary lull, the smoke from Mohamed's cigarettes would cross his room, the patio, and reach us conveying his confusion, his regrets and sometimes his sobs. Mohamed was finally talking to us! We thought of him as being very sexual, he was, in fact, first and foremost, a romantic.

Mohamed wasn't a bad father. He was a lover. And that justified everything in my eyes.

Back then, I was convinced that M'Barka was telling the truth. Saleh was just her cousin, no more than that. I couldn't imagine her cheating on my father with him.

Today, looking back, I tell myself that anything is possible.

II

—————————

He was here before me. Well before me.

He was born in the countryside around Béni Mellal two years after my parents' marriage. Their first child! A boy!

Family life started auspiciously. A boy, whenever he arrives, is a good sign, synonymous with good fortune, wealth, happiness.

He was the first born, indisputably the oldest child. M'Barka and Mohamed didn't hesitate long in picking out a first name for him: Abdelkébir. The servant of the Almighty! They knew, deep inside, that they would quickly have other children, other servants, but that this one would always be special in their eyes, the symbol of their family, of their future, their name kept alive for years to come.

Thanks to Abdelkébir, my mother, once and for all, acquired a legitimate place within the large Taïa family.

My father decided to celebrate this birth. Now he would really change his life, his days and his nights would no longer be the same. From now on, a new light would brighten his world in a thrilling, exciting, happy way.

A celebration, yes, a big celebration was in order.

At that time, Mohamed was still living at home with his parents, with his sister Massaouda, who would never marry, and with his older brother El-Bouhali, who had been married a long time himself. El-Bouhali had not yet turned against him. Later on, he would disown my father by claiming, purely and simply, that they didn't have the same father, that Mohamed, conceived in sin, had no right to any inheritance. El-Bouhali would keep everything for himself. Mohamed would find himself with nothing. For the time being, a certain unity reigned in the household. All of them were still more or less young and money wasn't their main obsession. All that mattered to them was pleasure, the pleasure of living, of making love, of eating. The pleasure of just being here, able to be happy together. Pleasure as principle, pleasure as guide.

M'Barka invited her whole village to this celebration. Everyone joined her to celebrate this new beginning in life. Only the family of her first husband, the one killed in the war, the family that had taken custody of her daughter Amina when she remarried, didn't show up, but that didn't surprise her. M'Barka had to invite them anyway. Fights between family clans, she had suffered from them for too long. Overflowing with joy, with optimism, she wanted to reconcile with everybody at this celebration. She forgot the bad things people had done to her. She tried to forget how easily and without remorse people do bad things. Obviously she was deluding herself. One person's happiness does not necessarily make someone else happy.

Mohamed bought a sheep, a cow, and a dozen roosters. He even wanted to buy a camel but M'Barka stopped him. She was afraid of the evil eye. She knew what certain women in the village were capable of. She suspected they would inevitably cast a spell on her. She was used to the jealousy of others, even of people who had nothing, and she knew how to distance herself from it.

Abdelkébir had to be celebrated. One had to give him a sense of joy upon his arrival in the world, but, at the same time, protect him.

Like all Moroccan women, M'Barka had her *fquih*, whom she could count on in case of danger. He was simply called El-Hadj, an old man known both for his piety and for his contact with the invisible world, the world of the *djinn*, and for his power as a sorcerer. She went to see him. He prepared the protective *hjab* she was to permanently leave around Abdelkébir's neck, especially during the celebration of his birth. He also taught her mysterious incantations and advised her to say them regularly during the celebration.

Everything turned out fine, in the end. Happiness came easily, seemed close at hand, eternal. Evil no longer existed. Sidi Molay Brahim protected them all, his *baraka* guided them.

Later, Abdelkébir was even granted a rare privilege: since M'Barka no longer had milk in her breasts, my uncle's wife, Fatéma, nursed him in her place for at least four months and, through this link, became his second mother. Several years later, when kids from an opposing clan took it out on me for the thrashing my clan had given them, slamming my head against a wall, and blood flowed incredibly red for a long time from the right side of my skull, Fatéma cared for me tenderly, putting sweet red pepper on my wound. Finally, to calm me down and stop my tears, she took her right breast out and put it in my mouth. I never understood this mystery: Fatéma always had milk in her breasts, even as an old lady. All my life I would remember the very sweet taste of her milk, its consistency, its smell that strangely brought to mind the scent of flowers in the public garden at Hay Salam. I can still see myself sucking like a baby, Fatéma's strong milk invading my mouth, my palate, my throat, my stomach, my intestines. I liked it. I love it: this connection and this liquid, this feeling of well-being and this love, this pleasure and this sorrow. I was eight years old when this double event took place.

Long secret, long delayed, the war between my father and his brother finally broke out. Mohamed and M'Barka, defeated, not knowing what to do when faced with such injustice, left everything and headed for the city, first to El-Jadida, then to Rabat, and finally to Hay Salam. Oddly enough, and I never knew why, my uncle's family, some time later, also decided to leave the countryside and settle in the same city we did. Just a thirty minute walk separates us from them. So, despite the problems, the resentment, the hatred and the unending disagreements, a semblance of normal relations was maintained between the two brothers and the two families. An Arab proverb says that blood will never turn to water. Isn't that the truth?

I never liked my uncle. He was dry, yellow. He doesn't look like my father. He is always full of life even though every time I get to see him, he gives me the impression that he's going to give up the ghost at any moment. And I wished for it more than once, this death, this final justice, this guaranteed appointment, this deserved revenge.

My father has been dead eight years already. El-Bouhali is still alive. A living corpse.

My uncle, and I have no choice but to think of him this way, betrayed everybody. Only a few months after Fatéma's death, he married this girl from the countryside who was the same age as his youngest child. He disowned her just five months later to marry a second wife, then a third. Islam permits you to take four wives at the same time if you want to.

Normally, I shouldn't have liked Fatéma either. I witnessed all the trouble and low blows she regularly dealt my mother. But I couldn't do that. I still have her milk inside me, still have the scar she cared for with sweetness and love. These things remind me of her tender gaze upon me and this special link that makes us one, her, Abdelkébir and myself.

Fatéma, for the others, was a bulimic shrew and a merciless witch.

I called Fatéma Mama.

Abdelkébir did too.

He's my brother! Yes, my brother, my big brother! He's mine!

I have a big brother … A big brother, for real! And his name is Abdelkébir. He's big. He's more than my brother. We have the same father, the same mother. He is the first-born son, I am the second.

Saying that to others, repeating it time and time again in my head fills me with pride.

It's childish, I know. For some people, it's even silly. I don't give a damn. That's how it works in my mind. When I think about him, I'm always the little kid, the one he needs to protect from life's dangers and he's always the great man I want to become someday.

My brother has been there from the beginning. He is the second head of the family. He studied Political Science at the University, read I don't know how many books. He worked because of us, not for himself. He helped Mohamed and M'Barka build their house in Hay Salam. He gave me books, his books, gave me music, his music. And most of all, he took me to the movies: discovering films changed my life, my way of seeing, and that's because of him.

I have a big brother. He has a moustache, a fine black moustache that makes him look important, makes him handsome.

I have a brother, and when I was little, we'd sometimes watch television together in his room. He would put me in bed with him so I wouldn't be cold. Under the same blanket, we'd spend hours glued together. One to the other. I forgot the images that paraded across the screen. In my heart, I still have that delightful sensation my little body felt when it came in contact with his, big and hard.

I knew his smell. I knew the skin on his face, on his ears, on his hands. I knew the small wrinkles around his eyes. I knew the way he breathed. I knew his silence.

Abdelkébir didn't speak. And when he did, he was like some prophet (a poet) who announces a new holy verse. Therefore I retained by memory and in my heart all that he said.

In his absence, I'd enter his locked bedroom via the window and I'd stay there for hours, sitting, or else stretched out and in a state of suspension like that I'd see what the room contained. Books, books, books and records. The little bed: our bed. The big but somewhat low dresser. The stereo system. Dirty clothes kind of everywhere. I'd bathe in Abdelkébir's strong scent, that manly smell of his that I loved, that I'd wallow in, that I'd mix with my own and breathe in deeply.

Like a little dog, I needed my big brother to play with, to sleep up against and sometimes to lick.

He hid his underpants under his bookcase, the ones that had a particular odor and were stained white on the inside. It took me a while to figure it out. It was his sperm.

Oh, yes, I even knew my brother's sperm. I touched it, studied it, sniffed it. One time, I almost even ate it. That sperm came from him. That sperm was him.

It seemed normal to me to feel that kind of desire for everything that had to do with Abdelkébir. And in my mind, it still seems normal. When it came to my brother, I didn't deny myself anything. Everything was natural. Everything about him suited me, touched me inside with force and delicacy.

And the end of each month, when he got paid, my brother bought us meat, lots of meat, and fruit we weren't used to eating: kiwis, mangos, grapefruits. My mother would prepare a special meal. Tagine with prunes, holiday style. Our stomachs full, we were happy, truly, for at least the course of an evening. Then we would pray for him. Sincerely.

I am moved to tears because I loved my brother so much. I am moved to tears because Abdelkébir brought me so much happiness. I am moved to tears because I have a brother like him who is there for us, for me.

We didn't have a bathroom in the house, only a toilet. Abdelkébir liked to wash his hair a few times a week. I helped him each time: I poured hot water slowly over his head as he bent over the kitchen sink. If I love napes today, it's because I spent such a long time looking at my brother's, long and thin. I often wanted to bend over a little further and kiss it tenderly. I wanted to reach out and caress it with my hand, gently tickle it and listen to Abdelkébir's laughter. I wanted to run my fingers through his hair, play with it, pull it, draw, scratch, dream … I wanted to do so many things when I was with Abdelkébir. I had no control. And I didn't resist.

I dried his hair and afterwards, fascinated, would watch him comb it, in a frenzy, forcefully. I stood in admiration before this exquisite mix of coquetry and virility.

Everything, everything, everything about my brother pleased and inspired me.

For Bread Alone by Mohamed Choukri, the book that introduced me to literature, that book was like him. Who else in our family, except Abdelkébir, could buy such a book and, because it was banned at the time, take the cover off and hide it under his bookshelf, in the middle of his sperm-stained underwear. I endlessly read and reread that novel about the terrible, hard life Mohamed Choukri had led in Tangiers.

My brother was my whole life when I was in Morocco.

He helped me form sentences, write letters. I cried over his words, thinking of him. He bought me a plane ticket, a sugar donut one night in the Rabat *medina*, a blue tooth-brush, white swimming trunks and a green winter coat that I still wear today.

One day he left. He got married. It took me a long time to get used to his absence. I never got used to it, really. I wasn't the only person in the family who felt this dreadful sorrow. I pictured him doing things with his wife and that disgusted me, made me furious. It was a betrayal, not on his part, but on the part of society: a man, a real one, was supposed to get married. Of course, he delayed this event as long as possible, but that only increased the sorrow when he became seriously involved in this other life. From now on, another woman, a foreigner, had him all to herself. When I was depressed, it made me feel like committing murder or suicide. Unable to kill the foreign woman, the enemy, I very seriously, solemnly promised God that I would never marry. I would keep my promise.

Abdelkébir changed, of course. With relish, the women in Morocco transform men into their slaves, their dogs. They brainwash them, trivialize them, kill them slowly but surely. It's their main task. Abdelkébir became someone else. I no longer recognized him. He no longer called himself Abdelkébir: his wife pronounced his first name with an exaggerated sophistication. She destroyed it, took away its charm, its power.

Abdelkébir was no longer the brother he used to be.

Summer, 1987. The end of July.

While waiting for the train to leave, Abdelkébir brought my little brother Mustapha and me to a café that didn't look like the ones in Hay Salam (too noisy, reserved for men only). It was the very posh Lina's Café. People didn't rush through breakfast. Everyone was dressed casually, elegantly: men, on their way to work, proudly wore short-sleeved shirts and linen pants. As for the women, they joyously showed off their flower print dresses and so seemed to fly far from their offices, out toward the sea, the beaches, to some mysterious rendezvous, with their lovers, to be sure. Abdelkébir ordered for us: three orange juices, two hot milks, one espresso, three little *pains au chocolat*, and two napoleons. A morning feast! His voice was firmer than usual. He took charge of the situation like a man, and that made me happy. He played the part perfectly and I was proud of him.

I don't know why he suddenly decided to take us on vacation. Back then, he was no more than a minor civil servant and he didn't earn a lot of money. Our sisters were left out of the trip but they weren't jealous: boys hung out with boys and girls hung out with girls. There was a certain justice in that somewhere! The girls would finally be free of us boys, from our watchful gaze which supposedly protected them from the outside world and its dangers. They could do what they wanted, without having to explain themselves or ask permission. It's hard for me to admit it but I was like every young Moroccan guy: I kept an eye on my sisters, considered it my mission. I was the guardian of their honor. I acted like a man, the kind of man people hoped I would become. Fortunately, that didn't last long. I gave up the idea of becoming that sort of man rather quickly after our trip with Abdelkébir.

For the first time in our lives we were going on vacation, together. There would never be a second time.

Tangiers. We would spend a week in this ancient international city.

Why Tangiers?

I didn't ask myself that: we were going on vacation and it didn't matter where. Marrakech, Esssaouira, Fez, what was important was that for once summer vacation didn't mean staying home and doing nothing, being home all the time, to the point of insanity. Now that Tangiers holds a special place in my heart, I wonder if my love for that city was born during that first stay, or, later on, when I went back there at age twenty. In any case, as we started this trip, everything I knew about Tangiers, and that amounted to almost nothing, would soon change. My vision and my idea of that city would be turned upside down forever. In my heart and in my mind, Tangiers will forever be associated with my big brother. Thanks to him, a new and other world opened up for me. I was both happy and afraid.

After the copious breakfast, we went back to the Rabat-Ville station to catch our train. On the way, I bought a small notebook to draw in. Why? I didn't know why. I don't remember. Maybe it was to imitate rich people's children.

In the train, on the spur of the moment, I decided to assign the notebook another role, that of a private diary. Really private.

Tuesday

We got on the train this morning at 9 o'clock. In the beginning, it was almost empty. Then, when it stopped at Salé and Kenitra, it filled up quickly. The compartment where we were didn't have a door and that worked out well because after just an hour into the trip, it got very hot and the whole train heated up like the *hammam* in Hay Salé on Thursday night, the eve of the holy day.

Mustapha, I'm not being fair, I know, but I don't remember what he did anymore, what he was like. When it comes to Mustapha, I often forget everything, rarely pay any attention to him. He's 10 years old, still a little kid. And me ... I'm going through the troubles and storms of adolescence.

Abdelkébir read for the whole trip, this fat novel with a title I couldn't understand, *Christ Recrucified* by Nikos Kazantzakis.

Abdelkébir, as usual, didn't speak. There's no conversation with him. He's there. You're there with him. In silence. You don't look at one another. From time to time he'd content himself with asking the question, "You OK?" Mustapha and I would answer together, the same way each time: "Just fine, big brother."

But for me, for a while already, I had made it a habit to secretly observe him. To study him from head to toe, let myself dissolve in him.

I journeyed across his body, seated right in front of me. For the entire trip. He wasn't aware of a thing. I had dissolved inside him and he never realized it.

Abdelkébir is 30 years old. He's a man. M'Barka, more than anyone else in the family, reveres him. For her, he comes before everyone else, and to prove it to him, she always saves him the best of what there is, the best of what she cooks. She loves him more than she loves us. And me, I also love him more than I love the others, more than I love anyone.

His reading absorbed him the entire trip. I tried to read, to guess from his face the story inside this novel with the enigmatic title. Nothing. Nothing was revealed. Is it a love story? A happy story? Sad? Tragic? A spy novel? Nothing. No sign that would let me guess the content of that book or what was going on in Abdelkébir's head.

That irritated me. The impossibility of knowing what was on his mind made me furious. I really felt like asking him to tell me the story that novel told but that was out of the question. With Abdelkébir this kind of closeness is inconceivable, an overly large barrier keeps us from talking like this, naturally, in a familiar way. With him, all words are reduced to a strict minimum.

But miracles exist.

"I'll pass this book on to you when I'm done with it … if you want," he said, as he continued on with his reading.

Surprised, disconcerted, I mumbled without thinking about what I was saying:

"It's too thick for me … lots of pages …"

Silence again.

He brought it up again a few minutes later.

"You don't have to read the whole thing."

"Then I won't know how it ends …"

"I'll tell you."

"Really?"

"Yes."

"But there's another problem … That novel is written in French, right?"

"Yes, so what's the problem?"

"I don't speak that language as well as you do."

"It doesn't matter if you don't understand everything. The important thing is that you keep moving, that you constantly keep reading a little bit more, a little bit more … And then one day, without even realizing it, you'll end up understanding everything."

"So when are you going to loan it to me?"

"In two or three days, maybe a little longer … I'm a slow reader."

That's it. A true miracle. A conversation with Abdelkébir. Well, the word "conversation" is a little exaggerated. Short sentences. And a promise.

We arrived in Tangiers around two o'clock. The station is located right next to the port and the beach isn't far away.

Abdelkébir had booked a room with three beds in an old hotel that directly overlooked the beach on the coast road … The Hotel Tingis. It's a real palace that's falling into ruin. You feel like you're on a movie set that isn't used anymore, scenery without life but full of ghosts.

This hotel frightens me a little. There are too many dark corners and it's almost empty.

After we put our things in our room, a vast, strangely designed room with a ceiling that was too high, we went out to buy sandwiches, then immediately came back to the hotel. We didn't meet anyone, neither coming nor going.

This hotel really scares me. I don't dare tell Abdelkébir. I don't want him to think I'm a wimp but at the same time I'd love him to take me into his arms to reassure me or else, if I admit my fear, to invite me to join him in his little bed, the way he did back in Hay Salam.

We ate our sandwiches (all tuna) in silence, and then Abdelkébir imposed a siesta—like M'Barka, for whom it was a sacrosanct habit. Without believing in it and without complaining either, Mustapha and I tried to do as he did. We are totally dependent upon him and consequently must obey him.

I love obeying Abdelkébir.

I didn't manage to fall asleep. Abdelkébir did, and very fast. He snored for a long time. And since that's what kept me from falling asleep, I watched him, studied his body once again. I had the bed in the middle. I rolled onto my right side, turning my back to Mustapha.

Abdelkébir was in full view.

It had been very hot. All he was wearing were these black underpants. He was sleeping on his back, without a cover. His body is light-skinned, really light. He has some hair on his chest, a lot on his legs and calves, very black and curly.

He's not very strong, even a little thin compared to other men from Hay Salam. But he is, without question, a man. All man: I don't know how else to put it. I know I'll never be a man like him, a man as real as the one he will become, more and more as years go by.

He was sound asleep. His snoring, like M'Barka's, didn't bother me in the end. His stomach, almost flat, rose and fell with a regular rhythm. And I rose and fell with it, hypnotized.

My brother's body was there in front of me all afternoon. I scrutinized it, studied it from head to toe with the great care of a scientist dwelling on every detail. The slender nose. The big eyes. The bushy eyebrows. The thick hair I washed so many times. The lips, full-fleshed and sensual. The thin moustache. The cheeks, not completely round. The neck ... The enormous Adam's apple. The gently falling shoulders. The not-really-muscular chest. The dark nipples. The navel ... The black underpants and what they concealed. The strong legs. The prominent knees. The calves, muscular, after years of cycling. The feet rather small and beautiful.

All afternoon, I swam inside this unconscious body, that couldn't know how it was entertaining me. This body that is a part of myself and, at the same time, is another self.

Later on, around 5 o'clock, Abdelkébir took us to the beach, which was swarming with people.

Around 8 o'clock we ate in a fancy restaurant on the coast road. I don't remember what we ate (maybe fish). I was tired and only wanted to do one thing: sleep. Abdelkébir understood that. He brought us back to the hotel around 9:30.

He's changing his clothes. He's going out again to walk around.

I'm busy reporting the day's events in my journal and wondering where he's going like that, all dressed up, more elegant than usual, so handsome, more handsome than usual.

All of a sudden, I'm not even sleepy.

Wednesday

I wound up falling asleep pretty fast yesterday, I think. I dreamt about Tangiers all night, Tangiers that I don't really know yet. I was walking alone down streets full of people, not just Moroccans, not really Moroccan streets. Tangiers belongs to another lifetime, one set in the fairly recent past but one in which I played no part.

When I got up, Mustapha was still sleeping. Abdelkébir wasn't in his bed. I immediately thought he had spent the night somewhere else. With whom? Where?

Suddenly he came into the room, a towel around his waist. He had just taken his morning shower and even at a distance smelled good, like his vanilla shower gel. He said "good morning" with a nice smile, forced perhaps, but one that basically translated an inner state of well-being ... and that really intrigued me. Without thinking, I answered with a question: "Did you spend the night here, with us?" My audacity surprised him. As a way of answering, he flashed me this half-smile which showed his amusement and, at the same time, his annoyance, and then he turned his back to me. He let the towel drop from his waist, revealing, almost proudly, his butt.

What a shock!

He had my mother's butt! Yes, I'd seen it before, several times in fact, very long ago, in what seems another century, when, as a child, she would bring me to the ladies' section of the public baths. I never really looked at them. Women would pass by and their butt come into view but it didn't bother me. Their breasts too, I know what they looks like.

My father's butt, no. Mustapha's butt, no. Not my sisters' either, no way.

Abdelkébir's butt was right in front of me, less than seven feet away. I could even (I dreamt about this for a moment) reach my hand out and touch it, feel it, get a better look. His butt wasn't fat, far from it. It was kind of oval, fleshy without being too full. Above all, it had character, which accentuated the few black hairs you could make out in the cleft.

I closed my eyes for a few seconds.

I slowly opened them again. My heart was pounding. I didn't know whether I was happy or scared, delighted or on the verge of a heart attack.

Abdelkébir still had his back to me. He had slipped on a pair of black underpants (the same ones he wore yesterday?). He was awfully sexy. I was proud of him. I was jealous too.

We spent the rest of the day at the beach, swimming, baking in the sun. Abdelkébir continued reading Kazantzakis's novel. Mustapha and I read too, comics in Arabic that he bought us yesterday. Tarzan for Mustapha, Rahan for me. I like Rahan, love him, more than Tintin, Superman, Spiderman, even more than Tarzan.

What I write in this journal makes me afraid. What if Abdelkébir reads it?

We're still at the beach. It's 4 o'clock. Abdelkébir is sleeping now, exhausted from the sun and from reading. Mustapha has made some friends: they're playing soccer together not far from here.

I'm lying on my stomach and I'm watching Abdelkébir who's lying on his stomach too. His butt, wrapped in that black bathing suit, continues to call out to me, irresistibly, and I don't know what to do about it. It's not that his butt is beautiful, it's just that it's part of Abdelkébir. This is insane. I'm insane. I've got to stop staring at it.

Impossible to think of anything else.

What is it I want?

Am I going to write down everything that comes into my head? Everything Abdelkébir makes me feel? And that buttocks ... His buttocks ... Oh, God! This is horrible! I'm so happy!

I'm going to try to sleep too.

Sleep, Abdellah, sleep! That's an order.

It's 20 after 12.

In the summer, the night never ends because it never starts.

After the beach, we went back to the hotel to shower and change our clothes. Then Abdelkébir took us for a walk through the streets of Tangiers.

First the new part of the city. We walked the length of Victor Hugo Avenue which was swarming with people. As on Mohamed V Boulevard in Rabat, people were stylishly dressed, especially the girls. You would have thought they were heading to some party. People in Tangiers seem lost to me, don't even seem Moroccan. Besides, most of them speak Spanish pretty well. We could actually see Spain from this kind of lookout point on Victor Hugo Avenue. It was getting dark, really dark in the distance. On the other side of the Mediterranean, you could clearly see the twinkling lights and this rather ostentatious signal station that seemed to flash its beacon, extend its invitation, while at the same time warning anyone who might try to cross the strait that the dangers were numerous and dreams could quickly be reduced to ash, lives broken forever.

I found this spectacle cruel. Sad and cynical. But I was certainly the only one who did. The passersby seemed content. Maybe their dreams were still intact, strong and luminous.

To have Europe right within your sights, forever: I couldn't stand it for long, I'd go crazy.

I told Abdelkébir how I felt. As usual, my effort to break the ice surprised him. He smiled shyly without looking at me. I immediately felt totally ridiculous. What I had said about that damned Europe over there, wasn't anything interesting. I almost had tears in my eyes, I was so ashamed.

Five minutes later, Abdelkébir surprised me by asking without even looking at me: "So, does that mean you wouldn't want to travel to Europe someday?" I answered in a flash, delighted to finally be able to interact with him: "What for? Everything that's important to me is here." I was being sincere. Mustapha spoke up in turn and answered Abdelkébir's question: "Me, I'm going to live in Spain when I grow up. Spain is beautiful, isn't it?" Abdelkébir concluded: "Andalusia ought to be beautiful, it's still part …"

The *medina* in Tangiers, even though it looks like the ones in Rabat and Salé, has something unique. You can sense danger everywhere and you sense it constantly. It might rise up at any moment and by its hellish movement carry you off into its dizzying chasms. All the traitors are in Tangiers. This fact is scary, of course, but it is also seductive, sometimes.

A shiver ran through my entire body while we were visting this *medina* which was bursting at the seams with people. Abdelkébir was afraid of losing us in the crowd. He offered me his left hand, the one near his heart, and gave Mustapha the right one.

That's when I had this really strong feeling inside: my body and my heart were linked forever to this older brother, so close, so present.

With Abdelkébir, life, even life lived silently, calmly, would sometimes throb with excitement. Become romantic. Unforgettable.

With Abdelkébir, I would always surrender my self, even among infidels. I don't exist for myself anymore. I exist for him, belong to him. My life is not my own.

Thursday

What was Abdelkébir thinking last night?

He woke us fairly early and announced our schedule: "Today we're going to Tetouan!"

Tetouan? Where's Tetouan?

I had no idea.

Abdelkébir explained that it was only two hours by car from Tangiers.

Why leave Tangiers? We're fine in Tangiers. We've just started to get our bearings and now we have to go some-where else. Of course, just for one day. But that's one whole day away from Tangiers, away from this hotel that I'm starting to like now. Away from the beach where we gladly offer our bodies to the sun. Away from a certain intimacy with Abdelkébir.

I was sad. Abdelkébir didn't notice. He seemed delighted, as if he were going off to meet an old acquaintance, a friend, a lover.

Just when I thought I was getting closer to Abdelkébir and little by little figuring out the mystery that is this man, I suddenly realized the opposite was true. I don't know how any of this works and there, right in front of me, stands this brother of mine who walks, who breathes. His eyes that can hardly look at me. And I have to do as he says without arguing. Be obedient, do everything his way and that's that.

I had a fit. In silence, obviously.

I have no memory of Tetouan. We got there late morning. We gulped down some tea in a downtown café then took another big taxi to El-Madiaque, a kind of smuggler's village where you could find anything, especially stuff that came from Europe.

I finally understood what Abdelkébir was after when he forced us to make this trip. He has always loved hunting for antiques and El-Madiaque is considered an antique-hunter's paradise. He could have said so right at the beginning, but, dictator that he is, a bit like my mother, he decides things on his own and then doesn't talk about anything until the very last minute.

I hate shopping for antiques. I make an effort, pretend to make an effort. Mustapha didn't have to force himself to go, he just followed Abdelkébir everywhere. They both got excited over items that left me totally indifferent.

They bought records, video cassettes, movie posters, posters with singers on them. A huge amount of spare parts to fix I don't know what. Glue. Old earthenware dishes and a nightgown for my mother. A huge amount of chocolate for my sisters. A suede jacket for my father. I had to pick something out too. Everything was cheap. I could pick whatever I wanted. But what? Abdelkébir kept at it. He insisted. Continue being the kill-joy? I didn't dare. So, to please him, I ended up buying a Best of David Bowie: I know he likes him and I do too, of course.

That's that. That's everything we did today. Spent hours in a car. Spent hours shopping. And back to the hotel, completely exhausted. Back to Tangiers.

I'm still not really over the whole day.

I felt jealous too. Over what? Over who?

At least I feel relieved to be back in Tangiers, back in this hotel room where Abdelkébir's strong smell has already impregnated everything.

Finally, I can breathe!

Friday

Abdelkébir has disappeared.

Mustapha and I got up pretty late this morning. Abdel-kébir wasn't in his bed. We thought he was taking a shower.

A half hour later, he still wasn't back in the room. So we decided to catch up with him in the shared showers next to the stairs. He wasn't there.

Where could he be? Having breakfast in the café next to the hotel? Without us? At the beach already? Gone jogging like he sometimes did in Salé? Reading newspapers in the main lobby?

It was Mustapha who first noticed, there, on the already made-up bed, the white envelope from Abdelkébir. He opened it. There was money inside, 100 dirhams, and a note written in Arabic that said the following:

Good morning,
I forgot to buy something important in Tetouan yesterday. I need to go back. I'll return this evening, maybe late. I imagine you can figure out how to keep yourselves busy while you're on your own. Go to the beach. Or else to the Mauritanya Theater, the one next to the entrance to the medina. *Here are 100 dirhams for the two of you. That should be enough to get something to eat. Be careful swimming, there are sometimes currents that can be dangerous … Only swim where you can touch bottom, not anywhere else. I'll be back this evening … perhaps very late. Don't wait up for me.*
Bye,
Abdelkébir

Mustapha got really excited over the idea that we'd be spending the day alone. Not me. What were we going to do without Abdelkébir? What decisions could we make without him? And how would we make them? Anyway, I couldn't imagine myself making them. Acting like a man already? No way! Taking charge of other people is just not what I'm about. Even making my own decisions is a big problem, a daily nightmare.

I don't like freedom.

I had this funny feeling that Abdelkébir's absence would haunt me, bother me all day long. And that's what happened.

I tried all day to picture him in Tetouan, in El-Madiaque, walking around, arguing over prices, looking for that all-important something that had forced him to go back to Tetouan a second time ... I couldn't do it. I could easily picture him there, picture his body that I feel I've almost memorized by now, but not the rest. Not that city which has come between us, that city which I don't like.

And what if he lied? What if he went there to meet some girlfriend? Some boyfriend? All of a sudden I didn't trust him anymore. Based on my suspicions, this incredible hatred toward him rose up inside me. I felt ill, unhappy, alone, sad, depressed, with no taste for life. Something inside me wasn't working anymore, wasn't working like it should.

Was that normal?

I finally admitted it, do admit it, don't know how to put it, can't say it any other way: I'm in love with Abdelkébir!

I'm not going to go into the nature of that love here. It's something beyond me. Something that haunts me.

I'm in love and that's all there is to it.

I feel abandoned. Unloved. Hollow.

Where is Abdelkébir now? What is he doing? Who is he with? What is he thinking?

On the beach, Mustapha caught up with his friends and played soccer with them all afternoon. They invited me to join them. Out of fear of making a fool of myself, getting treated like a girl again, I turned down their invitation and stayed by myself, offering my already darkened body to the sun.

This older man (maybe 35, 40?) came up to me. He gently touched my shoulder and said in French:

"You've got to be careful in the sun. It's dangerous. Do you have any sun screen?"

He didn't give me time to answer and offered me his. I rubbed it all over my body, thanked him, and gave it back. He started right in again:

"Your back. You forgot to rub some on your back. Turn around, I'll help you ... when it comes to your back ... it's hard to ..."

I did as he asked. He put his left hand on my shoulder and started to rub his sun screen across my back with his right hand. It didn't take long. Maybe a minute at most.

"What's your name?

"Abdellah."

"I'm Salim."

"Are you Moroccan?"

"Yes!"

"Then how come you speak French?"

"Because I live in Paris. I don't know any Arabic."

"You mean, you don't even know a single word in Arabic?"

"Well, maybe four or five ... tops ..."

"And you don't miss that ... speaking your country's language, your first country's language?"

"No, I really don't! How about you, where did you learn French?"

"My French isn't very good, I know that. I still make a lot of mistakes. I learned it in school, like everybody else."

"What are you doing here, alone in Tangiers?"

"Vacation. I'm on vacation with my little brother who's playing soccer over there and my big brother who's gone to Tetouan for the day."

"So you're alone then?"

"Yeah, you could say that."

"Do you want to go somewhere, just the two of us?"

"Where?"

"Maybe the movies."

"There's a theater at the entrance to the medina. It's called the Mauritanya."

"I know it. Do you want to head there and watch a movie?"

"Yeah, I'd like that. I love movies ... But there's a problem ... my little brother."

"He can stay here and play soccer. We won't be gone very long, two hours at the most."

"We'll take a taxi back to the beach."

"Alright. I'll tell him."

Saturday

I feel sick, sick, sick.

I am a traitor.

I have betrayed Abdelkébir.

At the movies, with Salim.

And the worst is that, I loved it, loved having this 40 year old man who smelled good wrap me in his strong arms and talk French in my ear while he tried to get at my penis, my ass. And I let him. And it didn't hurt. Oh, I loved it. Yes. Oh God!

I feel sick. I want to stay in bed all day.

Abdelkébir came up to me this morning. He bent over me, put his hand on my forehead. "Have you got a fever? Yes, you might have one, but it's not very high. You'd better stay in bed and rest. I'll go out and get you some Tylenol and some fruit. You need to drink a lot of water too. I'll leave my bottle of Sidi Ali next to the bed."

When he stood up, I noticed this hickey, this big red hickey where his tee-shirt usually covers his neck.

There it was, the undeniable proof. He had done the unforgivable. Him too. I knew it … I thought so … And I was right.

He had betrayed me too.

When all this started, I was a little nuts. Now, I'm completely crazy.

I feel sick ... Alone. Far, far from him who still remains so close.

Something has broken between us. Will it stay like that forever?

I'm going to try to sleep, try to forget if that's possible.

Forget what? Forget who? Can I forget a little, just a little?

Sunday

What happened to me yesterday? How did I get through the day? And the night? What did I do? Sleep? Did I sleep for twenty-four hours?

I don't remember a thing.

Abdelkébir was never far away. It was as if he had slept with me, in the same bed, like in Salé. Did he watch over me?

Today, oddly enough, I feel better. I'm fine, not sick anymore. Was I really that bad yesterday?

I am full of doubts, doubts about everything. I'm obsessed, consumed by questions without answers.

What was going on in my head? In my body?

It's all blacked out.

My first case of lovesickness. Sick because I was deceived,

betrayed, sick because I lost my head. You could call it a novel. I'm playing a part in a love story I haven't even read yet.

Abdelkébir, true to form, is silent. I know he didn't buy anything in Tétouan. He knows I know. Is he on to me? I hope he is. I hope he is suffering as much as I am.

Did I really see a hickey on his neck yesterday, a red mark, or was it only a dream?

I'm not sure about anything anymore. Everything's all mixed up. One thing is certain: my betrayal.

I have been punished. You have punished me.

There is some justice in the world. A one-sided justice. Abdelkébir wasn't punished. Fortunately not. Without him, we're lost in Tangiers. As soon as he's not around, we do the stupidest things. I do, anyway.

I'm disoriented. Out of balance.

We have two days of vacation left. Tuesday we head back to Salé.

Monday

Abdelkébir is in love.

Yesterday, for almost an hour, he raved about Tetouan. He has this dream that he'll live there someday, even buy a house. The Spanish side of the city is what he likes: its white color, its invigorating air, its separate status in Moroccan history … everything … he enjoyed everything about it.

Abdelkébir speaking! Now that's a real miracle!

When did he find time to fall in love? And who is he in love with?

Simple solution, I've just got to ask him: "Abdelkébir, my dear brother, are you in love?" But where would I find the courage for such a confrontation? What do I do now that I'm assailed by doubts, now that I'm furious, truly jealous? And what about Tangiers? What can I do about Tangiers?

At the moment we're in the kasbah. We're drinking black tea in tea bags, Lipton. I don't recognize Abdelkébir anymore. I mean like this, a man beyond shame and, since he returned from Tetouan, a man in love with this tea that I find insipid. He just said so. Said so again. He likes it like this. It's insane. He finds every way he can to talk about Tetouan. You can't shut him up. Real talkative.

He is happy. His face is radiant. His appearance is different, relaxed, not serious, cheerful.

From the kasbah, there is an extraordinary panoramic view of Tangiers, the port, the strait, the Mediterranean, the Ocean. The horizon. The future. The happiness life holds. The promises. Let's go for it! Really?

From what I can see, Mustapha doesn't notice a thing. Everything goes right over his head. He's still too young to grasp the complexity of things that happen around us. He's out of it, good for him.

Everywhere on Abdelkébir's body, I detect signs of happiness. Of love.

He's changed his cologne. The one he's using now is fruity. I'm sure he associates it with someone.

Hypocrite, do I dare ask him: "You smell good, Abelkébir. New cologne? Something you bought in Tetouan?"

I ask him. He looks at me, incredulous. Then he looks away without answering, which means he did give me an answer but without saying a word.

My heart is broken.

Tangiers is indifferent to my situation, to my unhappiness. I no longer know if I should love this city or hate it ... whether Tangiers is the start of some great passion or the start of some mutual hatred?

We are still in the kasbah. The waiter has put on some music. It's *Fatet Ganbenà*, this love song (all of his songs are love songs) by Abdel Halim Hafez composed by the gread Mohamed Abdelwahab. Abdelkébir seems to be enjoying it. He usually listens to nothing but the Doors, Jimi Hendrix, the Rolling Stones, David Bowie but here he is, Abdelkébir, savoring this marvelously famous and typically Egyptian ballad that tells the story of two friends who see this very beautiful girl pass in front of them. And once she's ahead of them, she turns around and smiles. The big question, the one that holds you in suspense throughout the song (even if you know how it ends), is: who did the girl smile at? At Abdel Halim Hafez or at his friend?

Fatet Ganbenà is very long, more than an hour long, but it never gets boring. Maybe this is the first time Abdelkébir has played it. You can see he wants to listen to it all the way through, find out how it ends.

He orders more tea. Generous: he calls the waiter back and asks him to bring us some pastry, and not just any kind, only gazelle horns will do. Reluctantly, Mustapha and I are celebrating something. Some event. At least it's not some catastrophe.

Is this the first time Abdelkébir has been in love? Did he make love for the first time in his life in Tetouan?

Can celebrating someone else's happiness have dangerous consequences for your own health?

And what about Abdel Halim Hafez, who I really like, should I start hating him now, now that he's celebrating Abdelkébir's love right along with him and showing no pity for my poor heart? His song *Fatet Ganbenà* is proving to be my enemy. An enemy who can turn up anywhere, follow me anywhere. Curse me. Put a spell on me. Hurt me. Blind me. Paralyze me. Assassinate me.

I am writing my loser thoughts down in this journal. Abdelkébir can hardly pay attention to us. He's totally into the song, taken over by the emotion it releases, the emotion it brings out in him. He's not here, not with us. With no remorse, he has abandoned us.

Fatet Ganbenà is ending. The really pretty girl has just told Abdel Halim Hafez that he, the handsome dark-haired man, he is the one she was smiling at. The audience interrupts the singer, shows him it's wild with joy. Abdel Halim Hafez triumphs. He's reached a state of osmosis with his public.

And right there with them sits Abdelkébir who is teary eyed now. It's a moment of celebration. Sad people, people like the singer's friend, people like me, we don't have a seat in that ecstatic crowd.

How sad and cruel happiness sometimes is!

And jealousy is sometimes legitimate, necessary!

Abdel Halim Hafez starts the last verse of his song again and the audience is delirious. Two, three, four times, he repeats what the girl told him: "It's you, my handsome dark-haired man, that I was smiling at."

The unthinkable: Abdelkébir is crying. He gets up and heads for the bathroom.

I close my eyes. Where does it come from, the darkness of the world?

Tuesday

It's simple.

Abdelkébir is in love, for real.

On the train heading back to Salé this morning he told us her name: Salma. He's made up his mind, he wants to marry her. This afternoon, the minute we get in, he's going to tell my mother.

Yesterday evening, he dragged us off to the *souk* where they sell jewelry. We spent hours there, looking at all kinds of rings. Engagement rings, obviously. Abdelkébir took a long time before deciding. Mustapha and I had enough. I mean, really, do guys care about rings? We would have pretended if Abdelkébir had explained why he absolutely had to buy one of those stupid rings in Tangiers and not someplace else. But, then he went mute again, as usual.

Yesterday I understood how selfish love can be.

Salma. No point writing down how much I don't like this name. I detest it. I hate it. I loathe it. I abhor it.

How can anybody decide to get married so fast? Has Abdelkébir turned into some kind of idiot now? The first girl who spreads her legs for him is the one he wants to marry! Even I wouldn't do that and I'm seventeen years younger than he is. I thought he was smarter than that, more open-minded, modern. Now I find out, he's not even old-fashioned. What a letdown!

I don't understand any of it.

What can I do?

I want to grab him by the shoulders, shake him good and hard, slap him twice, really loud, and finally kiss him, tenderly, on both cheeks.

I stay put. I don't move. It's enough just to be sad, watching him.

He still seems happy. I'm ashamed to admit it, to write it in my journal, but I feel like he's become a fool, a puppet, like someone's put a spell on him or something. He's making a big mistake: he's closing all the doors built into his future so that he can rush through the one that bitch Salma is holding half-open for him. He needs someone to save him, reroute him, to spring him from this trap.

When you're 30 years old, a Moroccan woman is inevitably a trap.

He needs someone to open his eyes. He doesn't need to thank this bitch for the cheap thrills she gave him by offering her life in exchange for his … His life, to be precise, is yet to be lived. Abdelkébir has gotten nowhere yet. Up to now, he's never been anything but a minor civil servant. Could he have given up his dreams just to have sex? And what about our dreams? The hope we placed in him? Our future linked forever to his?

I need to fight on his behalf, fight for him. And I know how to do it.

I'm going to lie to my mother, tell her that I saw Salma and she's a real bitch, a sorceress, a dangerous girl from the Rif who none of us could get along with. I'm going to do all I can to tell her to stop this miserable marriage. I know I won't have to give a lot of reasons why because she'll be on my side even before I start: Abdelkébir's wedding is not happening today and it's not happening tomorrow. My beloved brother's real wife is my mother, that's who, my mother and nobody else and she's the one who will choose for him when the question is seriously asked and all her conditions have been met, both by him and by the woman who would be his wife.

I am saddened, relieved. Happy?

I'm not going to cry.

I haven't been the same for a week now.

Abdelkébir's not lost. He'll still be ours for a few more years. That's what I feel deep down inside me.

In the meantime, I'm still traveling with him, moving across his body.

Tangiers, in the end, will prove to be all I thought it to be. City of my first battle to be loved. And I know I'll come out the winner.

Tangiers, city of every kind of trafficking.

Abdelkébir is lucky. His body belongs to us.

III

On the other shore, far, so far away, alone, helpless, panic-stricken, done for, I was already crying: "Help." I called Morocco, called my mother in Morocco.

I had just arrived in Geneva. I was still at the airport.

I told my mother a pack of lies. I had no other choice.

"Everything's fine, mom, just fine. Yes, I finally got here. Don't worry. It's not cold, not yet, anyway ... No, I wasn't afraid in the plane this time. There were a lot of Moroccans on board, I think that calmed me down a little ... Yes, my friend came to get me. He's here with me, we're still at the airport. I'll stay at his house tonight and maybe a few more nights. Yes, he's real nice, a real nice guy ... I promise, yes, of course, I'll tell him you said hello ... You'll say a prayer for him too? Well, of course I'll tell him, I'm sure he'll be glad to know that! Yes, mom, I told you, no, he doesn't take advantage of people ... and he's a really good cook ... He's got three bedrooms and plenty of blankets, so don't worry, I won't catch cold. He told me several times how he'd look after me like a big brother. I've got to go now, M'Barka, he's waiting, we're heading back to his place … I'll call you later … What's that? … What did you say? He's got a car … Say a prayer for me …"

September 30, 1998. Late afternoon.

Nobody was waiting to meet me at the Geneva airport. After two long hours, I had to face the facts: Jean's friend, Charles, wasn't coming to pick me up like he promised. He wasn't just late, like I had been hoping.

I called him at home several times. I got the answering machine every time: "You have reached Charles. You can leave a message, even two if that's what you want. I'll call you back as soon as I can. It's up to you." His voice was invariably the same, warm, too warm for a Swiss person. Charles had a voice like some guy you'd love to gossip with about anything and everything. An obliging guy, he would never let you down, no matter what. A good guy, a really good guy.

First message. "Hi Charles, it's Abdellah! I'm in Geneva … at the airport. I've been looking for you for fifteen minutes. I don't see you. Are you hiding somewhere? Where? Well, you'll probably turn up as if by magic … I had no problems at Customs … I'm here, waiting for you … I'm sure you're on your way … I mean, on your way to the airport … Maybe you're stuck in traffic … Anyway, I'm here. See you in a bit."

An hour later, the second message. "Hello Charles. It's me

again, Abdellah … Abdellah Taïa … the Moroccan … remember me? I'm still at the airport. There's nobody here now. I don't know where you are … And I don't know what to do … Maybe take a bus over to your place? Maybe you're sick, stuck in bed … so sick you can't even answer the phone. What should I do? What can I do? I don't know the code to get into your building. Okay, I'm going to wait a little while longer … I've got all the time in the world to wait … Kiss, kiss. See you in a bit, I hope!"

Another hour. Third and final message. "Good evening, Charles. Obviously you've forgotten me. You know, I sent you a letter a month ago from Salé to confirm the date of my arrival here in Geneva … Didn't you get it? … Maybe not … I probably should have called to tell you exactly when I'd arrive … You can't always trust the mail, especially Moroccan mail … Assumptions. That's what I've been under ever since the plane landed … I've been at the airport for almost three hours … I've got this really big suitcase. I have a few presents for you. I'm starting to get hungry. And I don't know where to go? Where should I go? You know I can't go to Jean's place. Besides, he's probably not even in Geneva. He's up in Leysin, in his chalet … I don't know what to do. I've got to figure something out. I was prepared for anything, except being abandoned. Abandoned? I'd better grow up fast, real fast. Thanks anyway … It's dumb, I know, but I was always taught to say thank you. So, thank you. Well, thank you for what? Adieu! as you say in Switzerland … Adieu!"

Three phone calls. Three messages. Three monologues. The next call is to M'Barka. She tells me it's already dark in Salé and Mustapha isn't back yet. The television is always broken. She's completely alone in that empty house. We're both alone.

Welcome to Europe!

I took the train to Cornavin Station in downtown Geneva. The ride didn't even take fifteen minutes. My mind was going blank. I couldn't think, didn't know how to link my thoughts, how to decide on anything. I only knew one thing: where to leave my suitcase. I'd leave it at the checkroom that most train stations have for baggage. Luckily I had some money with me, a few Swiss francs.

Geneva, that I really loved when I was with Jean, revealed a whole new side of itself: a cold city, colder than usual. Nevertheless, it was a beautiful city, more beautiful than ever, the leaves on the trees red, yellow, green, black, more full of color ... Geneva experiencing a magnificent autumn. And me, I just had to find myself someplace warm before night finally fell. No need to panic, be afraid, tremble, cry, feel sorry for myself about how things turned out. Now wasn't the time, no, no ... I had to be strong, STRONG. That's when I weighed 121 lbs. I don't know where my strength came from, how I found it in me. Undoubtedly it was the strength you find in sadness, the strength that comes with hopelessness: when you have nothing, you have no other choice. I let that strength guide me. I listened to it and it told me that all I had to do that night was just hang in there.

The Swiss Confederation had given me a scholarship. I came to Geneva to spend a year working on my post-graduate degree in 18th century French literature.

My father had just died.

Early April, 1996.

I met Jean in Morocco, in Rabat, at Mohamed-V University where he had come to participate in a seminar on "The Beautiful Lie."

The last day, right before the closing address, I innocently said to him: "I'd really like to meet you in the city later, have a drink, talk some more. Did you get to see Rabat a little?" He gave me a polite no that left the door slightly ajar. Without thinking, I stepped right in: "If you want, Sunday, the day after tomorrow, I'd be happy to show you around Rabat and, if you'd like it, Salé too ... I'm free all day ..." He liked the idea but only gave me a definite answer later.

As we were leaving the conference room, he came up to me and somewhat timidly said: "I'm not sure I'm free on Sunday. Tomorrow I'm going to Fes with some colleagues. We'll get back to Rabat late that night or else the next day ..." I didn't let him finish his sentence: "Here's my phone number, call me when you get back, even if it's very late." He looked at me, slightly amazed. I insisted: "Even if it's very late, trust me ... We've got a lot of company right now, relatives from the country and they stay up really late with my mother ... so, don't hesitate to call."

He took my advice. The next day, around midnight, the phone rang. It was him. He had just gotten back from Fes, which he loved. He was free on Sunday, all day. We decided to meet in front of his hotel at 10 that morning.

Something was going on between us, inside us, and that Sunday we spent exploring Rabat's sunny streets and monuments, crossing the Bou Regerg River in a *felucca*, strolling around Salé only went to prove it. A real understanding. One big intellectual collusion. A shared desire to laugh at the same things. A certain tenderness still in its beginning stages. Was it love? Perhaps. In any case, a strong attachment already, at least for now.

Instinctively, without thinking, I was starting to seduce him. I did a lot of talking. I showed off my culture, my knowledge of literature, movies. I called it my city, then my two cities: first Rabat, then Salé, then Salé and Rabat, then Rabat-Salé. I briefly recounted the history of both my cities. I was the perfect guide and my intimate and precise familiarity with even the smallest details of those places really surprised me. I felt like the king of Rabat-Salé. My palace was the casbah built by Oudayas. And next to me stood this Swiss man, yesterday, almost a stranger, and today a brother, a teacher, a boyfriend, perhaps, not yet my lover.

On the beach at Salé, I talked about Pier Paolo Pasolini, who had spent several months in Rabat during the last year of his life. This author-director fell in love with Salé at first sight. He even wanted to shoot a film there. He also wanted to convert to Islam. And it seems he would often come to the beach alone to watch the sunset, to the very beach where Jean and I stood watching it.

Several months later, Jean told me how moved he was by my Pasolini story, especially by the things I left unsaid but still made understood. In time, Pasolini would become our witness, the priest-*imam* who would bless our relationship.

As we were leaving the beach in Salé, Jean leaned his head in closer to mine and with his right hand caressed my shoulder.

I was surprised but not really surprised by this sign of affection.

I had won at something, won someone over. I felt proud without exactly knowing why.

On the *felucca* that brought us back to Rabat, we fell silent. We had said what needed to be said, perhaps a little more. In our silence we learned how to be really close.

It was en route to meet his colleagues from the University of Geneva, professors we were going to eat dinner with in Agdal, a middle class neighborhood in Rabat, that I told him this recent but important news: the French Department at Mohamed-V University had found me a scholarship to go to Geneva to complete my studies, but not right away, in just two years. At first, he didn't say anything for about twelve seconds that seemed like an eternity. Then he surprised me by running his left hand through my hair. Finally, and with great effort, he murmured: "*Mabrouke.*" I didn't ask who had taught him the Arabic word for "Congratulations." He was happy for me (for us?), and that was more than enough to fill me with joy for a long time.

He gave me his address and phone number.

When dinner was over, right in front of his colleagues, he kissed me three times, as they do in Switzerland to say goodbye, adieu.

He came to Morocco three times to see me. We visited three Moroccan cities together: Marrakech, Tangiers, Ouarzazate.

I went to see him in Switzerland twice.

We wrote each other at least five letters a week.

Here I am on the streets of Geneva. Berne Street. Neuchâtel Street. The Paquis district. The lake. Magnificent Lake Léman. France on the other side. I was going in circles. I bought a sandwich from a Lebanese guy, a chicken shawarma with a very strong, very garlicky white sauce that I can still remember. I didn't have enough money to get something to drink. A glass of water would do. And after that? After that: I'd sleep. But where? In a hotel? Impossible, I needed to save the few Swiss francs I had to pay for using the baggage checkroom. On the street? Next to Cornavin Station? Inside the Station itself? I ran all the possibilities through my mind. Go up to someone and ask him to put me up for the night (I'd seen that done so many times back in Morocco, why not here …)?

It was already nine o'clock. Darkness completely shrouded the city. The streets of Geneva were empty, worse than Rabat on a winter's evening. It was cold now. A crazy idea crossed my mind: go to a sauna and spend the night there. It's warm in a sauna. And a sauna would be open all night, wouldn't it? Jean brought me to one the first time I visited him in the summer of 1997. Just where was that sauna? I didn't remember any more.

So, forget the sauna idea. The street: no other choice. I started looking for a quiet spot, someplace out of the wind, if possible. Once again, my steps led me in the direction of Cornavin Station. The building was empty, silent, overly silent, sinister. The stores in the underground mall had closed hours ago. (In Geneva, everything closes at 7 p.m.—life just stops!) Fortunately, the store windows still had their lights on. I had a good time looking in them, especially comparing the prices for different items and then converting them into dirhams. I wondered what Genevans were up to at this hour of the night. I exited the Station via the main entrance and looked up at the windows of houses and buildings. Yes, lights were on inside them but I felt they were somehow vacant, the Swiss somehow mute. I searched for a human form, some sign, was only met with silence. And the silence in Switzerland is deep, opaque, deaf, horrible.

I needed to talk, to hear someone else talking. I didn't know what I needed to say. I needed to talk, just talk. After all, the Genevans spoke French and I spoke French too. Why had I studied this language for years in Morocco? Certainly not to be reduced to this silence. Before, I used to think that French was the best language for communication, a language that allowed you to express your ideas in a clear, precise way, achieve different shades of meaning, argue about things, defend yourself. I never imagined that French would become the language of silence. To say nothing, when one could be speaking French, seemed inconceivable to me, incongruent, even scandalous! One had to react, had to defend the honor of the French language.

Not far from the Station, there was a taxi stand. Without even thinking, I hurried toward the first one. The driver put his window down. To my amazement, he was smiling. He didn't give me a chance to talk. Before I could even say anything, there he was, right in front of me, talking in French. I was so happy to hear a few words in French, words pronounced with a Genevan accent, that I forgot I had to figure out what he was saying. I asked him to repeat what sounded like a question.

"I asked if you were Kuwaiti or Qatari?"

"Neither. I'm ..."

"Saudi then ... yes, that's it ... You have eyes like a Saudi. You're a Saudi. Tell me I'm right ... And you speak perfect French for a Saudi."

"No, I'm not a Saudi ..."

"I don't believe you. You seem so Saudi."

"No, not at all ... I'm ..."

"Don't tell me, let me guess! Are you from the United Arab Emirates?"

"No."

"From Bahrain?"

"No."

"Before I make a fool of myself, I give up."

"I'm Moroccan."

"I love Morocco! I love women from Morocco. Are you from Casablanca?"

"No, from Rabat. From Salé, actually."

To my great surprise, his attitude didn't change, he didn't become disagreeable. He certainly knew I wasn't the kind of person he was hoping to meet, the nationality he had expected.

He got out of the cab and invited me to sit with him on the hood, which was still warm. Like me, he just felt like talking. Like me, he couldn't stand the silence. He spoke more than I did, spoke for a long time. About the sun in Morocco. About this woman, Seloua, whom he had been in love with in Tangiers, this woman for whom he had been prepared to give up his life in Switzerland.

"She put a spell on me. I wasn't myself anymore. No woman ever made me feel like that. I had even agreed to convert to Islam so we could get married in Morocco. I used to dream of living with her in Morocco, in Tangiers, between the Atlantic Ocean and the Mediterranean Sea. Both of us at peace, living in another era. But she wanted to move here, dreamt about the stores, the cleanliness, how green Switzerland is, dreamt about the ski resorts. She had heard about Gstaad and wanted to go there. I told her it was no big deal, just some ski resort where a few wannabe stars that nobody remembers go to hang out. I told her Morocco was more human. Maybe some people there experience poverty but, in spite of everything, in that country there exists something more human, something more alive than what you find elsewhere. Humanity without western progress: that's how I saw Morocco ... That was ... fifteen ... fifteen years ago already. Fifteen years since last I saw the place. No doubt Morocco has changed a lot since then. She met someone else, a Swiss German. She broke up with me after that. I know she lives here, in Zurich, in Bern, maybe even in Geneva ... I don't want to see her again. I just want to remember her name ... Seloua, Seloua, a really pretty first name, so tender, so sweet. When I was with her, I always felt like I was tasting honey, that's how sweet her skin was, her smell too ... Maybe all of Morocco is sweet, overly sweet. That's all I have left, her first name and the way her skin tasted. And that's enough for me.

I'm happy I can tell you all this, it took me at least five years to put it all behind me. It's like she put a spell on me and then forgot to lift it after she broke up with me and started seeing somebody new. Later on I learned how important magic is for Moroccans, especially Moroccan women. I'm sorry I'm making you listen to all this ... I can't help myself ... I realize now how much my life is still turned upside down by what happened between her and me. It's like I've been damaged, permanently damaged ...

She wrote me a long letter. She told me she wanted money, for her, for her family. The extreme poverty, the hard life, she had enough of it, more than enough. She was beautiful, she knew it. That was her trump, the only card she could play to win over a rich man and, according to her, the Swiss Germans are all very rich. Anyway, the one she met was. I can't blame her, she was honest. She knew what she wanted.

She didn't dream about the same thing I did. That's what it was ... yeah ... that's what happened.

I wrote her a break-up letter of course, a long one. I never mailed it.

What did I say in the letter? I don't remember anymore. Nothing special, really. The same kind of things I always told her. How I loved her passionately. How I'd go crazy without her ... and I did, for a while, anyway ... I didn't send the letter. What for? It was already too late! In fact, when I look at the whole thing objectively, I understand her attraction to money, her desire to live somewhere else, somewhere far away ... And I believe she loved me because that's what I felt when we were in bed. And maybe that's what made me crazy: losing someone who loved me, who really did love me. She broke up with me because I didn't have money. It's as simple as that. Love is a rare thing. With her, I know it was love. For once in my life!"

He needed a minute to snap out of it, realize I was there, realize he had finished his story. I had given him my full attention. There was nothing else I could do for him. He didn't ask for anything else.

"Did you just arrive in Geneva?"

"Yes, this afternoon."

"You look like you might be a student, now that I see you up close ... Am I right?"

"I'm here to finish my studies in French literature."

"Do you live around here? I know there is student housing behind the Station."

"I don't have a place to stay right now."

"Are you looking for a place to sleep?"

"Yes ... but since I don't have any money ... It's just two days till I meet with people from the University."

"Where is your luggage?"

"I only have one suitcase. I left it at the baggage check room."

"I see."

"I can move and get around a lot easier without it."

"It's cold. Don't you think?"

"I think I can handle the cold ... no problem."

"That would really surprise me. Even for us Swiss, it's not easy."

"I'll find out. It still isn't that cold. It's only autumn."

"Listen, I don't want to offend you, but I think there's a Salvation Army not too far from here. You could spend a warm night there ... and for free ... They accept everyone."

"What is that, The Salvation Army?"

"It's an association ... a place where they help people who don't have money, don't have a place to sleep ... the poor ... emigrants ... political refugees ..."

"Do you think they take students too?"

"They don't care what you do in life. Just tell them your situation ... your story."

"That's all there is to it?"

"They know about people in need. I know it's behind the Station but I'm not sure where exactly. I'll ask the cabby behind me."

He didn't ask me to tell him my story. He figured it out by himself. I didn't need to say anything, to give myself away. I was grateful to him for that.

You had to follow the railroad tracks until you came to this little church, then make a right-hand turn, cross the square, and, there it was, several buildings, pretty basic structures: The Salvation Army.

"Life is unpredictable. Take care of yourself. And bundle up, it's just starting to get cold around here. Farewell! My name is Samuel."

I wasn't afraid anymore. I had forgotten about my life, my situation. All I wanted to do was find The Salvation Army. And get some sleep. And forget, forget about everything. Just stop thinking.

While I was walking through the public gardens, now in complete darkness, this noise made me jump. Was it a cry? No, it was the high-pitched laugh of some woman. Somebody was tickling this woman I couldn't see. Then she said something that played in my mind for hours: "Wait, wait, first the condom." I could guess everything from that, imagine everything, make a movie out of it. A love story in black and white, right there.

At The Salvation Army reception desk, this man with a shaved head sat reading a novel I knew very well: *Adolphe* by Benjamin Constant. He seemed like he was totally into it, captivated by the complex love story revealed in this book. For a minute or two, I stood quietly in front of him. Since he still didn't realize I was there, I had to disturb him, pull him away from his reading, bring him back to this other reality.

In a timid voice I said: "Good evening, sir."

He looked up, and, wow, what a shock: the man standing there in front of me was Michel Foucault. He did look like the French philosopher, looked just like him: his appearance, his shaved head, even the glasses. I was confused, excited. I was immediately taken in.

"Good evening, young man! What can I do for you?"

I didn't answer. He repeated the question a second time without getting annoyed. His voice was warm, a little out of practice, virile.

"Can you please help me?"

"Of course, what's going on? You look out of it, exhausted."

"I am ... I just want to sleep ..."

"That's all you want?"

"Yes, that's all. A bed is already asking for a lot."

"Well, you're in luck. We have several beds available tonight. I'm going to put you in your own room. You're not afraid to be alone, are you?"

"Yes, I mean, no ... no, I don't think so."

"Do you want me to put you in with someone?"

"No, no, please don't. I don't want to talk. I just want to forget. Forget where I am."

"I understand, I do ... Tomorrow you'll need to fill out some forms. Let me have your passport ... Don't worry, I won't steal it. Here's the key. It's Room 31 on the second floor. Good night."

I thanked him as sincerely as I could and went up to my room.

I was just starting to get undressed when all of a sudden this knock comes to the door. I put my shirt back on and went to open it. It was Michel Foucault. More shock, more confusion. He had a sweet smile as he whispered: "I thought you might be hungry so I brought you this cheese sandwich. I fixed it for myself in case I got … well, I think you need it more than I do. There are also two containers of plum yogurt, that's all they had left in the fridge. Now listen, try to eat all this before you sleep. It's not good sleeping on an empty stomach."

He knew just what I was going through.

With no warning, tears started running down my cheeks. And they were hot.

I put my head down. I really didn't want Michel Foucault to see that I was crying. I whispered the words "thank you" three times. Once again he wished me good night and reminded me that wake-up time was 7 a.m.

Marrakech. August, 1996.

It was hot. Too hot. People said this place was an oven in the summer and it really was! But that didn't bother me a bit. I was with Jean. Everything was going great with us. After Rabat, the relationship turned serious. Making love had a lot to do with it, but that wasn't the most important part, not for me anyway. I never said no to him. I was delighted to have a man of my own, someone who was interested in me, someone who got me out of my working-class world, at least for a little while, a cultured man, a Western man, in some ways the man of my dreams.

Yes, things were going great.

I told him about everything. My dreams. My secrets. My family. My reading. My shortcomings. My movies. I spent a long time talking to him about Paris because it had always fascinated me, because I hoped to live there some day. I shamelessly expressed my desire to become an intellectual, to be able to see the world more and more like an intellectual does, like he does.

Yes, things were going great.

One evening, Jean and I were out walking. We were walking around l'Hivernage, this chic neighborhood, before heading back to the hotel. All of a sudden, these two cops stopped us, even though they seemed very nice. They spoke to me in Arabic, spoke with a lot of violence and a lot of contempt: "What are you doing with this man? Why are you bothering him? Don't you know it's against the law in this country to bother tourists, you stupid …?" Unaware of the danger, I defended myself: "But I'm not bothering him. He's my friend." They shot right back: "Your friend or your boyfriend? Where do you think you are, in America? This is Morocco, you're in Morocco now, you ignorant piece of … you stupid fool. How much is he paying you? Let's see some ID and make it fast …"

Jean didn't understand. He spoke to them in French, told them I was his student in Rabat and we were visiting Marrakech together. They ordered me to tell him that what they were doing was for his own safety, his own protection, so he'd have a nice vacation, a good feeling about Moroccans, leave here feeling happy and come visit again, come back to see our beautiful country where he could always find someone to serve and pamper him.

I very reluctantly had to be the translator.

My identity card saved me. "Lucky for you you're from Salé. If you had been from Marrakech, we would have hauled you in right away … Go on, get out of here. And don't let us catch you around here again. Consider yourself warned. Move it …"

We started walking again, Jean and I, in silence. We started to hear these sounds, sounds that let us discern, there in the distance, the true soul of Morocco: Jamaa al-Fna Square, vibrant, ablaze, overflowing with joyous insanity. But who was being celebrated?

These two cops, just as they were getting back into their patrol car, yelled out from the other side of the street: "Make sure he pays you a lot ... and wash your ass good when he's done, dirty faggot."

Two young lovers, in a state of shock, saw the whole thing happen. They just stood there. For a couple of seconds, the boy stared at me in an odd way. The girl tried to make eye contact and smiled. Then the boy did too.

I didn't sleep that night. I cried my eyes out but found no comfort in tears. I don't know if Jean understood what really happened.

The next day, this brutal bell and this voice that sounded like it belonged to some boxer who was traumatized forever by his losses vigorously announced that sleep time, here at The Salvation Army, was over.

It was already seven in the morning. Back to reality.

It was still dark outside.

Michel Foucault had vanished.

A woman, small and somewhat older, served breakfast. She didn't say "Good morning," that wasn't her style. She passed out little trays and each one came with a big cup of very hot, plain tea, two pieces of buttered bread, some Laughing Cow cheese, some orange marmalade and a chocolate Mars bar.

No one said a word inside the immense room they used as a dining area. There were about fifteen of us, evidently of different nationalities. Since there were only three tables, there was no way to avoid each other but, sooner or later, we'd wind up looking at one another and then we'd look down, without a smile, without a friendly gesture. We were ashamed to be there. All of us already wanted to forget our past, forget last night, forget the troubles that brought us here and couldn't be shared no matter who asked. Each one of us had his story, his secrets, his tragedies, the parents he left somewhere else, the dreams he hadn't fulfilled yet, the love he could declare or not declare, his still raw wounds. Each of us carried his fate on his shoulders and though it wasn't too pleasant right at the moment, each of us tried to keep that flame inside us from going out, kindle that inner light that gave us the ability to live, to walk, to move forward regardless of setbacks, to earn some money and some of that happiness which we could (or thought we could) buy with a few Swiss francs.

It looked like I was the only Arab. Everyone else seemed to be from Eastern Europe or Asia. No Blacks.

At the most, the breakfast lasted fifteen minutes. You had to be off the premises by 7:45.

That meant a quarter of an hour to fill your stomach. A quarter of an hour to get yourself ready to leave this place, this place that despite everything did offer you some comfort, maybe even some warmth, before you had to face your immediate future: Where would you go? Where to spend the day?

There he was, at the door. Tall, strong, attractive, reassuring. Just the way I pictured a real man to be. Michel Foucault had reappeared. As people were leaving, he'd tell them: "Goodbye! Have a nice day!" Some of them said "thank you," others remained silent, probably because they didn't understand French.

It felt so good to run into him again, see this face I'd known for such a long time, meet this man constructed of words, words I first encountered in books and later in the love story he was reading, this man who stood there, already smiling, even though it was still dark. A man who wasn't dead, even if the real world said he was. I couldn't help admiring him. Loving him.

"Goodbye, young man! Have a nice day!"

"Thanks. You too."

"Aren't you forgetting something?"

"Uh, I don't think so."

"Are you sure about that?"

"Well … I think I have … all … my …"

"Think of your mother … what's the one thing she told you you should never lose?"

"My passport!"

"Right, and here it is!"

"Oh, my God, thank you, thank you! How could I have forgotten that? … I can't even prove I exist if I don't have my passport."

"Oh, come on now, you certainly do exist. I would be glad to testify to that fact if you wanted me to."

"How's that?"

"How's that!?"

"Yes, how's that?"

"Listen, have you figured out where you're going to sleep tonight?"

"Probably here, if you don't mind?"

"Okay, then. Tonight, after dinner, I'm going to show you how I would testify to the fact that you do exist. Run along now, I've got work to do."

"Good luck!"

"You too! And don't forget, dinner is served from 7 to 8:30."

"Thanks. See you tonight."

Tangiers. January, 1997.

His name was Mohamed. And, like so many others, he dreamt about leaving Morocco some day, for France, Spain, Germany, it didn't matter where, but his wildest dream was about going to the United States. He knew what he had to do, had even come up with a plan, a simple one, simple but effective: seduce a Western woman, offer himself to her, show her what a Moroccan man was capable of, in other words, fuck her like an animal, make her see stars in broad daylight, screw her nonstop, drive her wild, make her worthy of him, deserving of his cock. He wasn't afraid to talk like that, that was his big life plan, what he planned to do to make his life a success. Nowadays, he said, the only thing still working in Morocco was sex, sex, sex, and more sex, sex from dawn to dusk and all night too, sex everywhere and sex with everybody, even in mosques. Sex, he used to say, was the country's number one natural resource, its national treasure, its main tourist attraction.

But Mohamed wasn't lucky. All he met were hookers, sluts, bleach blondes, old ladies who wouldn't spend a dime, bitches worse than any Moroccan woman. Up until then, he thought Moroccan women were the world champions when it came to manipulating men and getting involved in every kind of sexual trafficking and, needless to say, magic. He was wrong. Women existed in other places, especially in France, who made Moroccan women seem as blameless as angels. No, he wouldn't go through with it, just made up his mind not to. From now on, he'd be careful around these witches regardless of their nationality, cautious around these infamous creatures, these Amazons untamed by faith or by law, wary now around this horror that he now named woman.

For quite some time, maybe about a month, while he was still waiting to meet a good woman, someone who knew how to be sweet, obedient, respectful, generous and sexy, he gave men a try. They were easier to satisfy, simpler to please. He liked being with them, fooling around with them, sometimes naked, but they didn't have to be. He'd let them suck on it. He'd penetrate them. He even imagined letting them have a shot at him. He wasn't afraid, he'd give them his private gift if taking a cock up his ass was a way to get out of this shithole country.

Yes, it was a fact, men were nicer, less complicated, more playful, more generous. They would spend money on you without counting every penny, spend more than they even had. It was that simple, really. Men came as a total surprise to him. They never interested him sexually before, but everything happens in its own good time, doesn't it? He played on their team now, had turned homosexual, but make no mistakes, only with foreigners. He'd never sleep with another Moroccan. Even the idea of being mistaken for a *zamel* in Tangiers filled him with horror. Besides, he was no *zamel*, no way. It was women he found interesteing, women who turned him on, and thanks to women, he still hoped to find a way out of this miserable country some day soon. That was the truth, the absolute truth. He wasn't lying. He was ready to swear to it on the Holy Koran, if that's what you wanted.

Mohamed talked a lot. He felt no shame. No embarrassment. He knew I was just like him, born in this bordello of a homeland, but that didn't stop him. He said exactly what he wanted to and said it all with lucidity, courage and sometimes even vulgarity. He was very moving, thanks to his beauty, his naiveté and his contradictions.

He was tall, light-skinned, brown-haired, always smiling, even when anger got the best of him. His eyes, his best feature, the thing you noticed right away when you met him for the first time, were very dark, immense.

Mohamed was handsome, really, really handsome. And even this adjective really isn't right enough or strong enough to describe how extraordinarily good looking he really was.

Jean cruised him in the Delacroix Arcade, the one at the entrance to the old part of Tangiers. And Mohamed followed him right away.

I didn't know what to make of this scenario: Jean, Mohamed and me.

Was this another reason Jean had come to Morocco, to get

laid by cute, young Moroccans? Hadn't he come to Morocco to spend time with me, just me?

A dark cloud settled over my head, a nimbus it was impossible to send away, impossible to put into words.

Jean paid for everything, for both Mohamed and me.

Mohamed was heavenly, sublime, someone I couldn't compete with.

I liked Mohamed too.

Jean invited him to have dinner with us. At the end of the meal, he slipped this two-hundred dirham note into his pants pocket.

Mohamed allowed himself to be bought. He didn't have a problem with that, obviously.

What about me? Was Jean trying to buy me too?

I didn't ask him that. I kept the question buried inside myself. Maybe he and I shared the same love of books, but we still didn't have the same set of values nor the same set of doubts.

I had no experience at all with money.

Thanks to his Swiss francs, Jean could have whatever he wanted in my country.

And, in a roundabout way, by watching how he behaved, here where everything was foreign to him, I learned, to my surprise, my curiosity and my horror, a certain fact about being Moroccan: I didn't want a single cent from him.

Apart from that, things were fine. At the end of his two-week stay in Tangiers, Jean invited me to stay with him in Switzerland the following summer. When he got back, he'd take care of all the paperwork so I could get a visa.

It was almost eight in the morning. It was still dark out. People like myself, who had spent the night at The Salvation Army, were nowhere to be found. I couldn't help wondering about them. Where had they gone? Off to work? Off looking for work? Off wandering about? Out stealing? Were they walking around in circles? Were they hanging out on street corners the way so many unemployed young people did in Morocco? Were they selling themselves? Were they dealing?

All around Cornavin Station, even though it was still dark out, there was a lot of activity: office workers headed to their jobs in Geneva, students taking busses to middle or high school, street cleaners hard at work, elegantly dressed women in sophisticated make-up, old people … Everybody seemed to know exactly where to go, what direction to go in, what bus to take, where to change lines, exactly where they were headed. The air held a certain energy, this excitement over being alive, over a new day starting. Of course, that wouldn't last long. Switzerland would always go back to being calm, return to its silence, its respect, its respect for everything, for every rule and regulation.

A day in Geneva. Alone. What would I do? How would I spend my time?

My body, well-rested, reclaimed some of its natural affinity for joy this autumn morning, its desire to be happy. Without even being aware of it, it was my body that chose to be happy. And I went along with that.

I headed for the baggage check room to get some clean clothes out of my big suitcase. I changed in the bathroom at the station, brushed my teeth, put on a little cologne to smell good. I was ready to meet the world and think about how I was going to spend my day.

The phone card I bought at the airport the other day still had some time left on it.

My mother? Should I call my mother?

Nobody answered at Hay Salam. M'Barka wasn't home. Where could she be? It was only 8 in the morning in Morocco. Was she still sleeping? Impossible, my mother had always been an early riser. So where was she? I needed her so badly, needed to hear her voice, even if the decision to leave her had been my own. Nobody there for me in Morocco? So soon? I was already out of the phone booth when I remembered her telling me the other day how she was going to visit my sister in Rabat.

Should I call Latéffa then?

"Hello, Latéffa? It's me, Abdellah."

"It's my brother. My baby brother. You left before I had a chance to see you."

"But I passed by your place two days ago in the late afternoon. I knocked and knocked but obviously you weren't home."

"I probably went to pick the kids up at school. You know, they're still not too good at finding the way back to the house by themselves."

"How are they doing? And how's that husband of yours, how's El-Mahdi?"

"Everybody's fine. We're all thinking about you and everybody says hi. So, how are you doing, way off in that foreign country where you have no *hbibe* and you have no friends?"

"Stop worrying. I've made a few friends."

"Well, that's a good thing. But nothing can take the place of your family, can it? Water is never thicker than blood ... We miss you already, honey. Mom says the house feels really empty now. She's completely alone. Mustapha is always out and Abdelkébir, well, you know Abdelkébir, he spends all his time with his wife. Mom will be here any minute now. She's going to stay with us because she can't stay by herself in Hay Salam anymore."

"I miss all of you too. It's cold here."

"Did you remember your winter coat?"

"Yes."

"Are your friends taking good care of you?"

"Yes, very good care."

"Don't cry. Sooner or later, everybody leaves. Today it's your turn. I know it's hard. It will take months, even years, before we understand how important leaving is for us and for a lot of other people … Don't cry … Be a man … Don't cry. Are you eating? You have to eat in a place like that, it's so cold."

"Latéffa!"

"Yes?"

"I'm almost out of credit. Give everybody a kiss from me. Take good care of mom. Tell her I'll call again …"

That Latéffa, what a sweetheart! Before Abdelkébir started working, she was the one who helped my parents provide for us. She made rugs, had a real talent for it. For quite a few years, you could count on having a nice dinner every Saturday because Saturday is when she got paid and she'd turn most of that money over to M'Barka. Latéffa was the first one to make sacrifices for the rest of us. She left home to marry El-Mahdi, this guy she loved who had a moustache.

Latéffa is the only one of my sisters who can make me cry. Her voice is so tender, so sweet, so filled with emotion, that I can't stop crying along with her whenever she starts to cry.

Latéffa always gives me the impression that she's in contact with another world. She knows what is really important in life, has come to understand love and suffering and has already forgiven everyone. I would have made my mother very happy if I had married a girl like Latéffa … if I had stayed there in Morocco. And it wouldn't have taken much for me to do that.

That morning, September 31st in Geneva, I had also lied to Latéffa on the phone. Some day I'd tell her the whole story. Talk about my life. Be totally honest. She would understand. She knows how easy it is to pass judgement on others. She wouldn't do that to me. I was sure Latéffa would accept me for who I am. Some day, Latéffa, it is I who will make sacrifices for you. You remember what happened to us that one day. We were both in the kitchen, everybody was taking a siesta. You had locked the door and taken me into your arms. You had something important to tell me. Something to do with love, of course. A tale of love. That was way before El-Mahdi. His name was Abdessalam and he worked as a foreman in that little factory where you used to weave carpets. You told me the whole story. I listened devotedly. When you were done, you took me in your arms again, kissed me on the forehead, then on the lips. Later on, I helped you get to all your rendezvous with him. We told M'Barka you were going to your girlfriend Najma's house. You should have married him. He came to ask for your hand and mom and dad hesitated a lot before they finally said yes. We were so happy for both of you. But our happiness didn't last long. Abdessalam's stepmother did all she could so that he'd marry her daughter. She put a spell on him, several spells. He never came to the house again. You cried for nights on end. During the day, you acted like nothing had happened because there was no way M'Barka could find out you were in love with him. You would cry at night. I would hear you. I couldn't do anything to help you, so I cried along with you.

After I hung up, I left the phone booth and ran for the bathroom inside Cornavin Station. I started crying again. In another corner of the world, there in Rabat, I pictured Latéffa crying too, crying just like me, crying, in fact, for me.

Nobody had died. Nothing had come between us. We were crying for what would later wither between us, collapse beyond our control.

Geneva was not Geneva anymore. The world was not the world anymore. Suddenly I was somebody else. I was weak. And I was strong and that was what linked me to Latéffa.

I walked without knowing where I was headed. That way I could just kept going, not have to think about where I might wind up. When I snapped out of it, I was surprised to see where I was: right across from the University, in Bastions Park, sad and magnificent in its autumn clothes.

I went to see Denise, the French Department secretary. I needed the address for the Scholarship Office and she was the only one I could ask. She gave me a cool reception, made it quite clear I was disturbing her. Her attitude, shocking as it was, really didn't matter. I got what I came for. I thanked her three, four, maybe even five times. Jean must have told her the whole story because all she saw in me was this piece of trash from Morocco who was about to blow into Europe. I had been transformed into this little demon, heartbreaker, arriviste, nothing but *a little whore* in the end. Even in her eyes, I was someone else. Not the person I thought I was. Every single person pictured me in his own way.

The Scholarship Office was on the other side of University Place, in the Uni-Dufour Building. At the reception desk, they told me where I might find Mrs. Weinstein, the woman in charge of my file. I knew she wasn't supposed to be back from her vacation before October 1st, but I had to take a chance that maybe she was already back. And she was.

Her office was a bastion of order and cleanliness. From the way the place looked, I was expecting to be met by some cold woman named Mrs. Weinstein. And there I was, standing in front of this petite woman, somewhere in her forties, with henna-red hair. And she was smiling, cordially too.

"Mr. Taïa? Ah! The man who holds the scholarship from the Swiss Confederation! But our meeting isn't until tomorrow … if I'm not mistaken?"

"No, you're right. It's just …"

"Well, whatever it is, you're here now, so, please, come in! And welcome to Switzerland!"

"…"

"Talk to me … Tell me everything … I want to know everything."

"Well, I got here yesterday, late afternoon."

"How was your flight?"

"Good."

"Are you afraid to fly?"

"A little."

"Me too. You know what I do so I'm not afraid to fly?"

"No, what?"

"Do you really want to know? Are you sure?"

"Of course, if you wouldn't mind."

"I drink alcohol. I'm always drunk when I get on a plane."

This pseudo confession was followed by this exaggerated, thundering laugh, the roar of some hysterical wild woman. Some crackpot. Was this really Mrs. Weinstein? Was I in the wrong office?

"Are you sure you're Mrs. Weinstein? Janine Weinstein?"

"Yes, yes, of course that's who I am ... and drunk as ever ... Ha, ha, ha, ha ..."

And drunk she was, it suddenly dawned on me. She didn't just drink up in the air, no, from the look of things, she drank down here on earth too, starting right off in the morning.

"Pleased to meet you, madame."

"Me too ... Call me Jo, everybody else around here does."

The telephone rang. She almost sang as she answered it: "Oh, hello-oh-oh.!"

I thought I was standing in front of Castafiore, the absurd and tender diva from the Adventures of Tintin comic book series. It wouldn't have surprised me if she broke into her theme song at any moment: "I laugh ... at seeing myself so beautiful ... so beautiful ... in this mirror ... in this mirror ..."

She didn't sing. She wasn't laughing anymore. The conversation turned serious. She tried to be serious. And that, apparently, took a lot of effort. She had someone important on the line.

Ten minutes later, she was still glued to the phone. The fact that I was standing there in her office had ceased to matter. She was looking out the window, kept turning her back to me and from time to time repeating the words: "of course, yes, of course, that goes without saying."

I told myself it was best to go. So I did. I waited another half hour for her at the reception desk.

When she didn't show up, I asked the secretary if she was still busy talking.

"No, no, she's done. You can go in now, but don't get upset if you notice anything strange. She's a little odd."

Just as I was about to knock, the door flew violently open. A volcano erupted.

"I don't have time to see you now. Come back tomorrow, no, make that the day after tomorrow. I've got to catch the next train for Bern. It's absolutely urgent. Adieu!"

I didn't even have time to come up with some kind of answer. She quickly disappeared, racing down the hallway like a nut in full crisis mode.

August 8th, 1997. The day after my birthday.

I left Morocco for the first time in my life. Jean said he'd come to the airport to meet me. He wasn't there. Instead he sent a friend of his. His name was Charles. Jean would join us as soon as he could, his train was late.

The first person I met in Europe: Charles!

He was kind, sweet, a little refined. He put me at ease right away. "I'm one of Jean's best friends, maybe his best friend ... but you'll have to ask him that." He laughed easily and, always the gentleman, I laughed along with him. Then, as nice as ever, he continued: "Jean asked me to entertain you until he got here. Can I get you something from the cafeteria?"

It was quite a while before Jean showed up. Charles used that time to ask me a lot of questions, first about myself, and then about how I came to know Jean in the first place, something Jean hadn't really talked about. I was delighted to answer his questions, happy to talk, to communicate, for as long as I could. I wanted to please. I did everything I could to make that happen.

As the minutes passed, this feeling of happiness (or something just like it) started to come over me. I was in Europe! In Switzerland! And just that thought, the realization that here I was on foreign soil, someplace that wasn't Morocco, that alone was enough to sustain my upbeat mood, keep me as happy as a child on a visit to the *hammam* with his mother, as delighted and amazed as some country boy who finds himself in the city for the first time.

"You seem young. How old are you?" Charles didn't believe me when I told him I was 23. He guessed I was five years younger. He went on to say: "That could cause problems for Jean ... When people see you two together, on the street, for example, they might think you're a ..."

He didn't have time to finish his sentence. Jean had shown up, finally! There was something unreal about seeing him again in a place that wasn't Morocco. I didn't know what to say. I found myself speechless. Grateful. Happy. Confused. I was also surprised, surprised to see him again, right there in the flesh, right there in front of me, right there, nowhere near Morocco!

And then the big question and all the other questions: Did he really love me? What did he really want from me? What could I really give him?

Yes, Jean had shown up late, but at least he showed up: my Swiss summer was about to begin.

I stayed with him in Geneva for two months, August and September of 1997.

It took us a while to get used to living together, a while for me to feel at home there.

Jean wasn't easy to live with. He was very fussy and had unbelievable mood swings. Almost every day, he'd get really irritated with me. I was terrified. I didn't talk back. I didn't cry. He had something in common with my mother: very strong dictatorial tendencies. As the days went by, I realized he wasn't a bad person but rather the product of a certain kind of upbringing, something and someone it was too late to change. I never felt at home there. No matter what it took, I had to adapt myself to his personality, his tempo.

Sometimes I was afraid: Switzerland struck me as a very strange place, much too quiet. This soundproofed country.

I figured out two other important things during this first trip to Europe. First of all, I realized to what degree my fascination with Western culture was based on reality. And then, once I lived there day in and day out, I got to see just how different the West really was, nothing at all like the place I read about in books or saw in the movies for so many years.

I came from another world and nothing let me forget that.

Jean wanted to expand my cultural horizons by taking me to museums and art galleries. No persuasion necessary, I was the one who wanted to, who felt a need to look at everything, discover it all. It was with him that I first saw paintings by Picasso, Goya, Holbein, De Chirico … art you don't forget. And that's how Jean, day by day, left his mark on me. He exercised considerable influence on my artistic tastes and opinions. All I wanted to do was learn.

And there he was, this college professor, right beside me day by day. He was brilliant. His enormous talent for seeing beyond things fascinated me. He needed to be loved and, at the same time, admired. I greatly admired him and I did love him, in my own way.

One day, in a restaurant, while he was in the bathroom, this elegant, slightly arrogant man in his fifties came up to me and gave me his card. He had written on it: "I pay very well."

So that's what Charles was trying to tell me, that unpleasant truth, and having it handed right to me meant I couldn't ignore it. Charles knew some people might think I was just some trick Jean was treating to a vacation. That's what he wanted to tell me, was all set to tell me when Jean showed up that day at the airport. For a lot of people, and the man who had just handed me his card only went to prove it, I was nothing more than a prostitute, some kind of cheap hooker. Making the rounds with Jean, being part of this "new" scene, meant a lot of people saw me as the object of his desire. What else could I be? After all, he was the one paying.

And anybody could buy me, just like he did.

I didn't cry. Tears wouldn't solve anything. I didn't understand what had happened but became aware of this new aspect of myself, a reality beyond my understanding.

Deep inside me, this irreparable fracture opened.

Several weeks later, the plane that brought me back to Morocco was full of Moroccan women trying to look chic. They were very expensive prostitutes. The high season had just ended in Switzerland and they were coming back to Morocco in triumph, their pockets full, their liberty, thanks to all those Swiss francs, finally paid for. Over there, just like back home, everything was for sale.

It was almost noon.

Everybody in Switzerland eats lunch at exactly twelve o'clock. I did the same thing, slowly biting into the Mars Bar they gave me that morning at The Salvation Army. It certainly wasn't enough, but the thought that I'd be getting a decent meal at the end of the day made being hungry bearable.

Mrs. Weinstein was still on my mind and I realized that meeting her had done me a lot of good, even though she was unaware of that. I found her entertaining, atypical, different, really different, from the way I pictured the Swiss in general. The fact that maybe she was a little crazy, a little "odd," as the secretary put it, was fine with me. The fact that she was, no doubt about it, hysterical didn't bother me either. In Morocco, almost all the women were like that.

Bastions Park, the place I went back to after seeing Mrs. Weinstein, was quite beautiful beneath the autumn sky. It wasn't cold and a bright, soft sun lit up this part of Geneva. Not a cloud on the horizon to alter this light. Not a hint of breeze. A soothing calm reigned over this park where people came to walk around, read, eat, sleep, admire the sculpture of the Four Reformers and cruise. Right in the center, there was a small fountain. I was thirsty. I went over to it to get a drink. I put my head down and that's when I first noticed how much it looked like the beautiful Wallace fountains they have in Paris. When I looked at it again, it did look like a Wallace fountain but unlike the Parisian ones, which are green, this one was painted black and I wondered what made them change the color. I was happy, got a little kick out of the fact that I could recognize a fountain like that, had actually gotten to see one for the first time in my life.

When I thought about it, I realized I was back in Europe, would get to stay there awhile and, just like in my dreams, was not that far from Paris. My life was changing. I was becoming this whole other person, someone I didn't even know yet. And I would get to laugh, cry, learn things, like things, disappoint people, disappoint myself, make mistakes, get ahead no matter what, make something of myself, do it for myself, later do it for my family, sing, dance, be alone, be around new people, panic, shout, make love, run, die a little, fall down, out myself, sleep, wake up, feel very cold, wait for the sun to return, finally get to see snow. Best of all, instead of just reading movie reviews, the way I did in Morocco, I'd finally get to go to the movies and see the actual films. I would get to write about my life, my past, my future, write it all down for myself and for others.

My future in Europe, a future that began at The Salvation Army, suddenly seemed so ornate next to that black

Wallace fountain. What a distant, almost here, terribly exciting future.

I wasn't afraid anymore. The dream I had was so sweet, I thought I saw angels. The angels back at The Salvation Army.

I had drifted off.

When I snapped out of it, I realized the Park was almost empty. Lunchtime was over and people were heading back to work. Geneva was drowsy and seemed to need a siesta. I did too.

It hadn't turned cold yet. The sun still caressed the city in its delicate light.

I stretched out on the bench. And I closed my eyes.

For the first time in my life, I slept right on the street. But not for long.

When I woke up half an hour later, my body felt lighter, relieved of who knows what, confident, in a good mood. It wanted to have some fun, keep things light for a while. So I decided to do some window shopping.

Not far from Cornavin Station was la Placette, this enormous shopping mall that really intrigued me. You could buy anything in that place, anything you wanted. On my way there, I passed this movie theater that advertized as its coming attraction the André Téchiné film *Alice and Martin* with Juliette Binoche and I passed the Payot Bookstore, a place I visited with Jean on several occasions the first time I stayed with him. One of the entrances to la Placette looked out on this very pretty square that had this very Swiss fountain that I really liked right in the center of it and the whole thing seemed unreal, like some kind of architectural model.

On the ground floor, they have this huge bakery, the most interesting one I know. It's a friendly place, maybe even the friendliest place in all Geneva. You can watch the baker do everything, nothing is hidden from view. It's entertainment, theater, a *souk* where frenzy and noise are not against the rules. That bakery, with all those smells that make you feel so hungry, and all those bakers dressed all in white, immediately restores your existence and your destiny. Happiness, it seems, sometimes starts with a good crisp loaf of bread. Who could ask for anything more?

One day, right there in la Placette, Jean bought me a blue sweater. And before returning home at the end of my first trip to Geneva, I bought chocolate there for the family. My first camera came from there, another gift from Jean.

The further I moved inside that gigantic mall, the more I remembered details like these.

Details I didn't mind.

That afternoon, there were a lot of people on the second floor. All the shelves were well stocked. Clothing, furniture, books, CDs, perfume … You could find everything you needed to live the good life, all you needed were pockets bursting with Swiss francs. I moved from one window to the next, attracted, in spite of myself, by all this opulence, curious about everything, reading the labels and brand names on everything they sold, naively imagining the day when I could buy anything I wanted. In my mind, I entertained this image of myself as some kind of crazed consumer. And happy to be one.

I ran into these women dressed totally in black, women from the Persian Gulf veiled in their *abbayas* and doused with sweet, very strong perfume. They seemed to know their surroundings perfectly. They were completely at home. They took their own sweet time, tiptoed around like cats lifting their enormous, intriguing, monstrous derrières behind them. I followed them for quite a while, without knowing why. I wanted to grab some part of them but the darkness of their *abbayas* precluded any communication, any contact.

I left them in the Fabric Department and left la Placette. It was still light out.

Once again, I had to decide where to go.

Just as I was asking myself that question, I realized this guy had been following me for a while. He seemed in his forties. He motioned for me to stop. When he caught up with me, in that cold voice that people used to giving orders always have, he said: "Follow me."

Where?

Why did I follow him? Was he somebody else who thought I was a hooker? Probably. I found him physically attractive so I followed him, silently. I was also curious. Curious to find out what it felt like being a prostitute.

He led me, in total silence, to this place I hadn't discovered before, a place not far from la Placette: the public toilets. Once inside, I realized this place was all about something the rest of Geneva didn't have: intense poetic sexuality.

A dozen men of all ages were lined up in front of the urinals and were lovingly looking at cock.

That really struck me. It wasn't like I was shocked but more like I had just caught up with a bunch of my old friends.

These men expressed their desire without becoming violent, touched the penis in a very gentle, courteous way. Inside this dirty, underground location, they played out a sexuality that was both clandestine and public. They smiled at one another like babies. They didn't talk. Instead they let their lucky bodies do the talking for them. They would masturbate with their right hand while touching their partners buttocks with the left. These men were not paired up. They all made love together, standing up.

My forty-year old, always the man in charge, didn't let me enjoy this scene for long, this display that finally showed me the human side of the Swiss. He grabbed my arm and yanked me into a stall. He slammed the door behind him and got right down on his knees. Slowly, carefully, he unzipped my fly, gently pulled my penis out and popped it into his mouth to get it up. He could really suck cock, sucked so well I forgot to pull out before I came. He seemed enraptured and swallowed my sperm, every last drop of it, with his eyes closed. Then he got up, wiped his lips and chin with his handkerchief, kissed me on the neck, on both cheeks and the lips. His strong, manly scent swept right over me. I closed my eyes so I could identify it later, stored it deep inside me, in my stomach and in my heart. He stuck his right hand in his jacket pocket and pulled out an orange. An orange! He gave it to me, and this time his voice was completely tender, drained by pleasure: "Thank you. I pass through here every day at about 6 o'clock except weekends. See you tomorrow!"

And he left.

And I lingered a while in the stall, pulled myself together, took stock of what just had happened with this man. Afterwards, the pleasure I got from holding that orange under my nose and smelling its exquisite sweetness made me shoot again.

I was happy, thanks to a moment's pleasure, relieved. When you come right down to it, he didn't take me for a prostitute. He liked me, wanted to get a taste of me, that's all, that's all this was about. Nothing but a mutual exchange of pleasure.

How did he know oranges were my favorite fruit?

Ouarzazate.

I really didn't know Morocco. I knew Salé and Rabat. Tangiers less so.

Jean gave me a chance to learn something new about this country, let me broaden my concept of "Morocco," discover other aspects of this "enchanting" country, to quote the travel ads.

The last time we saw one another was in Morocco.

Ouarzazate. Early February, 1998.

We forgot about any tension we felt back in Switzerland. Forgot our differences. Our fights.

All we felt now was the pleasure of being together again. Determined to be happy together for a couple of days there in the South.

Spring had come early and the almond trees were already in bloom, large, thin, majestic almond trees scattered about the land. I was seeing them for the first time in my life, and their beauty, which really jumped out against this ochre, desert landscape, profoundly moved me. I couldn't help sharing these feelings with Jean, again and again, at least twelve times a day. After a while, he'd get sick of listening to me and then he'd reprimand me in such a kind and serious way that a lot of times I wouldn't even answer him. I knew his annoyance was only half-real and basically felt he was just amusing himself; I amused him and somehow this made our last trip to Morocco light; really enchanting. The kasbahs we found and admired almost everywhere in this region, small kasbahs, large kasbahs, architectural masterpieces, cliché images of the Moroccan south, really made a very strong impression on us. We would visit them several times a day, in silence, in reverence, and we loved everything about them and everything about ourselves when we stood inside them. We were in this lighthearted mood and it drew us closer together than ever before. Yes, we were there for one another, there in that place so far away from everything, from every familiar landmark. Once again, we would laugh at the same things. And at night, back in our hotel room, we'd make fools of ourselves, give running commentaries on TV programs and then we'd make love for hours.

The night before we left, we watched them hand out the Césars on TV5. I was mesmerized by movies, spellbound by them, and Jean knew this and gladly shared in this magnificent obsession. He'd listen while I revealed my dreams about films, about movie stars, while I went on and on about my favorite one, Isabelle Adjani, talked about her beauty, her talent, her background, and her films. He wasn't especially fond of that actress, but for my sake, whenever I referred to her so ardently, he'd be in the same passion over her as I was.

In Ouarzazate, it was already spring, springtime all around us, springtime to revive us and Isabelle Adjani went everywhere with us. I was her agent, her biggest fan, her lover. For the first time in my life, I finally had somebody I could talk to about her. And because he was such an attentive and, at the same time, entertained listener, Jean was more than up to hearing every detail of this dream that had overtaken my reality.

For ten days, Ouarzazate became our love story, a book with a happy ending.

I knew how my day would end: Michel Foucault was expecting me, along with the others, for supper at The Salvation Army. Night was not far off.

Before heading back, I took a walk around the University of Geneva Library.

In the entrance hall, I ran into Jean Starobinski, the great Swiss writer, critic, professor. My admiration for him knew no bounds. He silently walked right past me, made no noise, emitted no sound. The way he walked was unobtrusive and his whole body, so full of life and young despite its years, moved exactly the same way. I wanted to go up to him, touch him, remind him that Jean had introduced me to him the first time I came to Geneva. I didn't, of course. I stood there petrified, embarrassed, shy and delighted by this coincidence. I watched him walk in right in front of me without recognizing me, cross the foyer, wait for the automatic door to open by itself, walk through it and disappear from my field of vision.

It was a sign. A positive sign that I totally accepted. Starobinski. A man of letters. A generous human being. A smuggler. Perhaps the last man who still snuck books across borders.

The reading room was almost empty. An odd handful of people labored there in monastic silence. In my mind, those people symbolized every student and well-read person's dream: to be passionate about some field of study and then find the ideal place to pursue it, go into it deeper and deeper! And that library, beyond any shadow of a doubt, was more than the ideal place to satisfy their thirst, their passion for learning.

I was only passing through, revisiting those walls where my turn would come to study for hours on end, become familiar with the books, the atmosphere there, the objects, the chairs and tables, the lamps, and the faces of the different librarians too. And finally with the card catalog room.

That room was empty. At least, it seemed empty. I headed toward the files labeled "R" to find some books on Jean-Jacques Rousseau.

I thought I was the only one in the room. Suddenly the thud of someone sliding a file drawer shut on the other end of the card catalog made me jump. I looked up. There was this man standing there, a little ways off, standing there staring at me. I couldn't really make out who it was. I looked down, then right back up. No, it couldn't be, it just couldn't be. But it was.

That man, who kept right on looking at me, was ... Jean. Even when I recognized him, I couldn't quite believe it.

He had changed. No, he hadn't gotten thin, scrawny. Now he had this goatee, kind of ridiculous since it made him look much older. He had aged in just two months. He seemed sad.

He was in shock.

I was too.

I knew I'd run into him again, sooner or later (no way around it: he taught in the same department where I had come to pursue my studies), but not that soon, not by accident, and not that day, especially not that day.

He continued staring at me, incredulous.

My eyes filled with tears. I wanted to run up to him, throw myself into his arms, let it be like old times again, lean against him and cry, cry for both of us, and then, he'd run his hand through my hair just like he used to do. I was the one who'd left, the one who broke up with him. I was the one who chose to move far away, but not that far … Seeing him that day, so near and yet so far, made me realize how much tenderness and attachment he aroused in me, and, despite my best efforts, always would.

He was a short man and that came as a surprise, since I hadn't noticed it before. He was really sad, but that was normal.

He started coming towards me.

I yelled out: "Not now, please, not now. It's too soon … or maybe it's too late. Not now."

He stopped short.

I turned around and ran for the exit.

I ran for a long time.

The streets of Geneva were empty again, just as dark as last night. People had put in a days' work and now they were back home, locked up for the night, comfortable in their own solitude, sitting there in front of the television.

After dinner, I went to see him. He was at the reception desk finishing the last few pages of *Adolphe*.

"Can I interrupt you for a second ...?"

"Sure, what's going on?"

"Well, maybe it's a dumb thing to say, but I think you look an awfully lot like Michel Foucault ... the philosopher."

"Do you think so, do you really think so?"

"Yes, you look just like him, even your glasses."

"Should I take that as a compliment?"

"I would. Michel Foucault was a great writer, a courageous and admirable man."

"So, it is a compliment then ..."

"Yes."

"But, how do you know I'm a courageous and admirable man?"

"I don't know … You seem like … like … well, you seem like someone people could depend on."

"How flattering!"

"Well, that's the feeling I get from you … a certain sense of security, of protection from …"

"What are you afraid of?"

"Afraid of? … Afraid of life … like everybody else."

"Not true, everybody isn't afraid of life."

"Do you really believe that?"

"Yes … Look over there, do you see those three Russians who sat with you during dinner? They don't look like they've ever been afraid of life. They look pretty tough to me."

"Maybe I'm wrong … maybe they've completely fooled me …"

"But what is it you're afraid of? To say you're afraid of life is both precise and vague at the same time …"

"I'm afraid of the sea because I almost drowned one day …"

"And that's it?"

"I'm afraid I made the wrong choice … Maybe I would have been happier if I had stayed back home in Morocco … Allowed my mother to plan my life for me, let her do everything, as usual … as always."

"And whoever said you could only be happy if you let your mother run your life?"

"Just having her around. Being with her, knowing she's there, close by. It's reassuring, even if you don't think about it."

"It's hard to be apart in the beginning, that's a fact. Then you get used to it, you do. You get used to everything."

"I disagree …"

"Well, you don't always have to agree with me."

" …"

"And now, since you've run out of things to say, off to bed, it's late … And if anyone asks me who you are, I can testify to your existence, even prove it. I am not Michel Foucault. But, like him, I do love books. Go to bed now. Let me finish *Adolphe*."

"See you tomorrow then … Goodnight!"

"Goodnight! … Listen, there's a surprise waiting for you in your room. You won't be alone."

The surprise was Tunisian. This guy, who seemed kind and sweet, was lying on the bed next to the window reading the sports section. He spoke first.

"Good evening! I'm Samir, from Tunis. You must be the Moroccan guy?"

"Good evening! You already heard about me?"

"Yes, thanks to the man at the reception desk."

"My name is Abdellah."

"How do you do? … He was right."

"Right about what? What did he tell you?"

"Oh, nothing, nothing … Just that we looked a lot alike. And I think he was right. You could pass for my younger brother … When did you get here?"

"Yesterday. And you?"

"This morning. And I already feel like I totally understand just how Swiss society works."

"How?"

"This afternoon, I was walking around downtown, waiting for The Salvation Army to open ... I noticed right away that everything here is very tidy, well planned, thought out, that nothing is left to chance. Even if you want to cross the street, there's a button that lights up this little crosswalk man. I watched several people push it. I wanted to imitate them, start right off by obeying the law in this country. Here's what happened: the light was red for the cars, but strangely enough the crosswalk man didn't light up for the pedestrians. To get him to change to green, I pressed the button one time. Nothing happened. I pressed it a second time. Nothing happened. I thought he must have fallen asleep. I didn't get it, nobody could move, no pedestrians and no motorists. I was annoyed and hit the button a third time, then a fourth ... and a fifth ... And to my great despair, nothing happened. Suddenly, from the other side of the street, this big ole woman starts shouting: 'Hey! YOU! You push it one time and then you wait. You're not back in the boondocks anymore.' I was so ashamed. I put my head down and imagined the people next to me were laughing at my stupidity, roaring at my ignorance. And then, when Mr. Crosswalk finally deemed us worthy to cross, that same big, fat lady crossed the street and yelled out the same comment or something just like it. I let her do it, understood that here in the land of the rich, every citizen is a policeman. Better get used to it. I'm warning you right now."

"Welcome to Switzerland."

"Thanks!"

Before I climbed into bed, before I let my safe, warm body drift off into sleep, I pulled the orange out of the inside pocket of my jacket where I had carefully hidden it.

"How about sharing this orange with me?"

I was the one who showed up late that time. A whole day late.

Right next door, France was celebrating its National Soccer Team's latest win, the World Cup, and it was loud and unbearable. One big happy country! That's what was depressing. Collective joy is always a little forced, always unsatisfying, always tiresome.

I felt like crying. All week long. Every night.

Five months after Ouarzazate with all its happy times, there I was back in Geneva for the second time in my life.

As soon as I got there, all hell broke lose between us, once again. Jean, me and hell, and summer hadn't even started yet.

In bed, next to Jean, in his apartment in Geneva, I wasn't asleep. He, on the other hand, was already snoring. The tears wouldn't come. Didn't come.

It was over. I could see it. I didn't cry. I stayed dry eyed and in that dryness rattled a certain kind of selfishness, me, me, me ...

Tears could have moved me to pity, allowed me to do something, take some step, extend my hand to touch this sleeping man from Switzerland, to touch Jean, this person I suddenly didn't know, wake this stranger, hold him in my arms. All our problems would cease to exist, all discord just disappear and he and I would be connected, linked together by a certain idea about love.

Tears like that never fell. I prayed they would. Then I prayed they wouldn't.

Jean? I resented him. I hated him. I didn't talk to him about anything anymore, not about me, not about my dreams, not about my family, not about Paris, a city he never really liked anyway.

I felt alone, abandoned, and yet there he was, right next to me.

I was afraid too. Of him. Of everything about him.

Right from the start, in Marrakech, he talked to me about freedom, about how free I was when it came to him. He told me we would be friends, not slaves to each other. I was younger than he was, and it was normal for me to take advantage of life and the pleasures it had to offer. At my age, he'd done the same thing: enjoyed life. That's how he saw things. We really were free.

Freedom, it turned out, was just a word. I wasn't free. All of a sudden I knew that, realized it in a brutal, traumatic way.

That second stay in Switzerland was very short. Very short and very intense. A Douglas Sirk melodrama. I was going through a breakup I couldn't handle. I knew I was making a radical decision, totally unaware of the consequences. I was just like my mother: I didn't know how to talk about things. Betrayed, I said nothing. Faced with Jean's silence, I became a chasm, an abyss, a nonexistent person. A shadow of my former self. Already out of there, already somewhere else. I couldn't stay.

My older brother Abdelkébir had given me the money to go to Geneva and see Jean again. I spent three days on trains: Rabat-Tangiers, Tangiers-Algeciras, Algeciras-Madrid, Madrid-Hendaye, Hendaye-Paris, Paris-Geneva.

I was happy as I traveled back to Jean.

On the boat that goes from Tangiers to Algeciras, I met Matthias from Germany and Rafaël from Poland. They were both my age, 23. They wanted to make a day trip to Tangiers but the Moroccan police turned them away because people of Rafaël's nationality needed a visa. Matthias could have gone there by himself, as Rafaël suggested, but he preferred staying with his friend and gave up Tangiers to be with him.

It didn't take me too long to figure it out: Matthias was madly in love with Rafaël.

On the boat, they kept looking at one another. Smiling. They didn't have to talk.

Matthias seemed shy. He almost never talked.

Rafaël was outrageously handsome and sexy: he knew it and loved every minute of it. His mouth was incredibly large and epitomized everything he stood for in life: greed and insatiability.

That night, on the train to Madrid, we got to know one another. We talked in English, eating tuna sandwiches. We had the compartment all to ourselves, just the three of us. We talked for a long time. Around midnight, just when we were supposed to get some sleep, the moment arrived, the single moment I think we all were waiting for, happened just like that, unplanned, no warning, and we took off our clothes and started to make love, all three of us naked together.

We didn't sleep. The hot night kept us awake, ready for love and its pleasures.

We were happy. Young and happy. The Spanish landscape hung like a frame around what surged within us and what we shared. Spain, the land of some of my ancestors, the land I set foot in for the first time in my life. Spain, still Arab in certain places, despite the centuries and all the destruction.

An hour before we got to Madrid, where I would have had to change trains, Rafaël suggested I stay with them a little longer, one more day. A whole day and night in Madrid!

I didn't know the Spanish capital.

I accepted.

I changed my train ticket without a problem.

I left Jean a message on his answering machine to let him know I'd be getting to Geneva a day late and that I'd explain why when I saw him.

Rafaël had gone off to look for a youth hostel close to the downtown area.

Matthias and I waited at the station for two hours. Two hours to really get to know one another. Two hours to become really close, become friends forever. Two hours that ended up with Matthias breaking down.

Matthias was crying.

I held his hand. I didn't know what to say to him. I knew why he was crying.

He was in love with Rafaël who wasn't in love with him. Rafaël wanted everybody and everybody wanted Rafaël.

Rafaël was an angel, a devil, a wonderful lover, a manipulator, eccentric, fragile, egocentric, cruel, innocent, perverted … but, most of all, Rafaël was extremely handsome.

Matthias would have done anything for him. Even marry him. Rafaël stayed with Matthias but wasn't really in love with him, he just liked him, that's all. He needed Matthias for his papers. An immigrant to Munich, he needed someone to help him get a residency permit, find a job. He also needed a place to sleep. Matthias did everything for him, out of love for him. And this unreciprocated love and the fact that the object of his affection was around him on a daily basis were a source of happiness and immense suffering for this Munich native.

Moved by this suffering, I held Matthias in my arms. Then he had a good, long cry, like a child. I wiped his tears with this big white, embroidered handkerchief my mother gave me one day and kept promising him I'd never wash it. His love for Rafaël had something strong, pure, holy about it.

Is the person in love the one with all the rights?

Maybe the answer is no. But love, once it reaches such a rare and lived-in state, deserves our prayers and our indulgence.

I loved Madrid. I loved being part of Matthias' love. I loved being surrounded by two warm, naked bodies, by four hands caressing me. I let them have me, in the afternoon, at night, in the early hours. I forgot about anyone else, thought only of them, there with me in that city, guiding me, leading me around, smiling at me. I had fathomed the secrets of their relationship, the depths of their hearts. I was them. I lived for them. And all three of us, by sharing this sensual and sexual love, became blood brothers, sperm brothers, far from our own borders.

As soon as I was back with Jean in Geneva, I rushed to tell him all about my beautiful adventure, all of it. I shared everything: how we met en route, my pleasure, my emotion, as well as my comments about their love. My joy at rediscovering with Matthias and Rafaël a kind of sexuality I had experienced in childhood and early adolescence. Group sex.

I must have overflowed with enthusiasm, too much enthusiasm, seemed absolutely delighted by the beautiful gift life had just granted me.

Jean completely changed right after hearing about my trip.

Was it jealousy?

Right there in front of me stood another Jean. All his shortcomings were exacerbated. Now he was foul-tempered.

Possessive. Grumpy. A killjoy. Insulting. Selfish. Noncommunicative. Insulting.

He ignored me. In his eyes I no longer existed, and yet I was more dependant on him than ever. He was the one who payed for everything. And he constantly brought that up.

I was suffocating. Jean had only one response: he withdrew further and further into himself, intensified the sad look on his face and hardly ever opened his mouth, except to say hurtful things.

After a few days, I stopped trying to figure him out, stopped trying to understand his love, his way of showing affection. All I could feel was my own suffering. I was inside a prison, more and more inside a prison.

Freedom in the West? What freedom?

One morning I got up early, well before Jean, and I wrote him a long letter that explained how living with him like that was more than I could stand. I didn't understand any of it. Love was certainly a complex emotion, and I didn't always understand it, especially when it took on these somber tones, this oxygen-robbing silence. I couldn't stay there. I had to leave, go somewhere else, breathe again, make sense of it all, and, especially, think about my future. What we shared together in Morocco and in Switzerland would always remain alive and powerful in my mind. He would always be the first one, the initiator, the master I would have to surpass in time. The very embodiment of love?

Charles, Jean's friend, lent me the money to go back to Morocco.

I knew that two months later I'd be coming back to Geneva to finish my studies, that I'd be away from Morocco for a long time.

Charles promised to pick me up at the Geneva Airport on September 30th.

In Morocco, one month before my new departure date, Marc, a friend of mine who taught at the French School in Rabat, someone Jean hardly knew at all, got this letter from him, warning him how "evil" I was and telling him to be careful because Abdellah was really nothing but a whore, like so many other Moroccans, a cheap hustler who had no scruples, a real lowlife, nothing but ungrateful scum. A terrible person. A heartbreaker. An egotistical loser who wasn't worth your time. A monster.

These were the words I had in my head as I boarded the plane for Geneva, that cold, other world where this huge battle needed me to show up, so it could start. I thought going to live in Europe would mark the end of waiting and waging battles within myself. I was wrong. I would still live for quite some time in obscurity. I would have to make radical and immediate decisions very fast, take my stand, distance myself further and further from people I loved, stop crying once and for all, manage my anxiety and my panic attacks. Forget about taking it easy. Learn how to love again. Let Jean play a new part without letting him take over my life. Reinvent myself despite any misgivings. Get ahead on my own. Be happy on my own. Frequently vanish. Decide to drink or not to drink wine, to eat or not to eat pork. Little by little, reexamine my views about Arab culture, Moroccan tradition and Islam. Lose myself entirely, the better to find myself. To summon, one gray and very cold morning, an army for my own salvation. It wouldn't happen overnight. When this Great Battle started, the angels and the faithful (the Muslims?) would be there at my side. Then, like cowards, they would abandon me. But in the meantime, I will have become stronger, definitely leaner, and perhaps my dream of being an intellectual in Paris will have become a reality.

ABOUT THE AUTHOR

Abdellah Taïa (b. 1973) is the first openly gay autobio-
graphical writer published in Morocco. Though
Moroccan, he has lived in Paris for the last eight years.
He is the author of *Mon Maroc* and *Le rouge du tarbouche*,
both translated into Dutch and Spanish. He also
appeared in Rémi Lange's 2004 film *Tarik el Hob*
(released in English as *The Road to Love*).